A Dream of Destruction

"Speak," the red man commanded.

The drums had fallen silent, silence taut as a bow string.

"I see streams of running red. There is a battle and death, the trampling of feet in wild flight, the sound of guns, the rattle of swords! Men stumble and fall and do not rise. Their blood reddens the thirsty soil. Listen, O warriors of the West gathering to your own destruction."

"Have a care, Witch," he warned thickly. "A flase prophetess shall die. Make sure that you interpret truly what my people dream."

"As water falls so do men. Out from leaden clouds is death. Its thunder was in your ears and in the cloud was reflected the red of blood."

Frantically, the dancers raised bare arms. "We have dreamed also, O Bear of the White North! Let the Sorceress explain our dreams!"

FLAME IN THE FOREST

Al Cody

MANOR.
BOOKS
INC.

A MANOR BOOK

Manor Books, Inc.
432 Park Avenue South
New York, New York 10016

Copyright,©, 1977 by Manor Books, Inc.
All rights reserved.
Published by arrangement with the author.
Printed in the United States of America.

ISBN CODE 0-532-15287-5

A MONTANA STORY

Chapter One

The Concord squeaked and rattled, showing scarred and rusty. Dust spurted up from pounding hooves, enveloping the coach, blanketing the horses in a mixed coat of grime and sweat. It swirled over and about Dave Drew, hunched like a gnome on the box, and set the flabby joweled drummer beside him to coughing and swearing. Inside the stage, sifting through every crack and crevice, it worked to make everyone outwardly alike.

The big man on the right-hand side, riding backward, differed from his fellow-passengers in that he was uncomplaining. To curse the driver, the horses, the uncomfortable sway of the broad leather suspension, or the road, might relieve one's feelings but in no way did it abate the physical discomfort. Mr. Abbott would have preferred the spare seat on the box but that had been preempted.

Abbott by itself was not a betraying name and the newness and quality of his suit was a far cry from chaps and high-heeled boots, crowned by a big hat — or, as so often seemed to happen, forced to go hatless when some such misfortune as a bullet through its crown spoiled the Stetson. When the passengers had first embarked on the run for the west, the drummer had grinned and spat, summarizing with a single word to his seat-mate:

"Dude."

Overhearing, Abbott had come as close to a grin as he ever did. He was attempting no disguise; on the other hand, if he could travel unrecognized, while about this business of an uncertain, not to say chancy nature, it could do no harm and might even help.

His eyes matched the summer sky. The fresh sprout of beard after scrape of razor showed a carroty tingue rather than going along with the brown hair above. The sometimes betraying limp, a reminder of a once savage wound, had gone unnoticed when he'd climbed aboard the Concord.

Fort Orme should not be too far ahead. It would make a welcome break in the steady monotony of travel. Except for brief stops to change teams and occasionally alter the human freight cramped inside, the stage had held a steady pace for the past fifteen hours, alternating to some extent for the last few minutes as it followed the turns and twists of a narrowing, ever more precarious trail, winding through a deepening canyon.

A giant spur of gray stone upthrust like a gaunt skeleton. Swinging around the barrier, the coach came to so sudden a stop that for an instant Abbott surmised that a road agent, or even a team of outlaws, might be meeting them, looking along leveled rifles and voicing a demand for material goods. The squeak of consternation from the flashily clad man seated opposite showed that he was not alone in that guess. Abbott revised his earlier estimate. Perhaps those rings which bejeweled the fellow's fish-belly white fingers were real rather than fake.

There was audible relief as such fears were dispelled by sight of a big wagon, athwart the road ahead. It sprawled like a wounded behemoth, blocking the narrow way. Others were on either side, freight wagons heavily loaded. The three had been pulled by a jerk-linestring of a dozen horses, still hitched to the immobile wagons. Abbott opened the door and reached the ground with the easy shambling walk of a bear. Wheels and weather had gouged a hole in the road. That, in combination with a dislodged stone from somewhere above, thick as a strong man's torso, had lifted and then dropped a wheel of the overloaded wagon. The load had slowed and slid as the wheel collapsed.

Apparently the mishap had occurred only moments before their arrival. The jerk-line operator, a lanky individual clad in the discarded butternut pants of the lamented Confederacy, topped by a faded blue jacket of the Union, had descended from his perch on the lead wagon to survey the damage. Having found it fully as bad as he had expected, he was relieving his emotions with a picturesque description of the road, its impediments, the horses and wagons and conditions in general. Beyond that he had done nothing.

"It's a plumb hell of a note," he pointed out plantively to his gathering audience. "And Blackjack ain't going to like it. Not him. He'll blame me, o' course. He always does."

That would be Blackjack McQuade, the sutler at Fort Orme. Logically enough, the supplies on the wagons would be consigned to him.

"And what with the blasted Indians turning rambunctious and all, he'll want these goods some sooner than usual, or even quicker," the driver added on a prophetic note. "Though what in tarnation I can do — "

Clearly he was inadequate to the demands of the occasion, and the others were no better. Resignedly, Abbott assumed charge. There would be no supper before they reached the fort, and as always, he was hungry.

The driver had hardly exaggerated the problem.

Not only did he carry no spare wheel, but even had one been at hand, to remove the broken one and replace it, with the weight of the laden wagon pressing heavily on the sagging axle, would have taxed the ingenuity of an expert.

Abbott made out a scattering of trees, scrub fir and cedar, a little farther along the canyon. Pressed as to what cargo he carried in the wagons, the driver remembered a consignment of tools. Among them were saws and axes, together with a surprising number of carpenter's hatchets — odd freight for a land with few builders — or perhaps not so strange.

Moving other goods piled above to come at the tools, Abbott's attention quickened still further as he lifted along with sweating and disgruntled companions, moving a long wooden box which might in a pinch serve as a coffin. On its side, someone had chalked the contents, harness. And possibly it might indeed contain leather goods, but any horse or team upon whom so hefty a burden might be placed would be hard put to sustain it.

Abbott kept his thoughts to himself, but his speculations received equal exercise. A sutler to whom such freight was consigned might bear watching — which obviously was not the case at Fort Orme. Which argued in turn a sloppiness of command.

Putting his shoulders into the swing of an axe, he felled a tree, then stripped it of its limbs. Carrying the long pole under an arm as though it was not at all burdensome, he fixed the smaller end atop the front axle of the crippled wagon, roping it snugly in place. The butt dragged well behind, the sagging weight of the new one-wheeled rear axle suspended upon it. As many as could found holds and lifted, and the broken wheel was removed. However ungainly, the repair held the wagon in place.

Goods were reloaded, the wagon dragged back in line, then the patiently waiting teams moved the barrier out of the stage's way. Abbott found a small reward, securing the seat on the box beside Drew.

His attire had suffered in making the repairs, stained now like his hands with grime and grease. Eyeing him with fresh appraisal, Drew's accolade was brief but comprehensive.

"You look like a tenderfoot — or did. Only you ain't."

They emerged from the canyon into a widening valley. Stockade walls showed in the distance, long since weathered to a matching drabness with prairie and sky. The post gave an illusion of slumbering, forgotten, but that gave way to stir and activity on its far perimeter as they wheeled closer. Revealed, the road on to the west was almost clogged with a motley assortment of vehicles, mingled with horsemen and even cattle, all heading for the fort, being received, swallowed up within the maw of the stockade. Drew's jaws, endlessly busy around a cud of tobacco, froze to immobility.

"Trouble!" he pronounced, and spat, so manifestly nervous that the tobacco was expelled along with the flood of brown juice. "Damn!" he added, exasperated. "Wonder what in tunket's stirred our noble red brothers to wavin' the warbonnet?"

Abbott's eyes took on a gleam, whether of expectancy or excitement, Drew was unsure.

"Would I detect a note of sarcasm in that comment?" he asked.

"Havin' a good pair of ears, you just might," Drew conceded. "But it ain't all for the Indians. We pale faces get spooked just as quick! Observe how everybody's peltin' for the safety of the post — they hope! Like there was a cold wind blowin' out of the west. Wonder if that red priest has found the sorceress he's been huntin' for — Satan's red-haired squaw, from all accounts."

His searching survey returned to his companion, between hope and question.

"You'd maybe know which end a gun shoots from, now?"

Abbott's thoughts, dwelling on that strange reference to a squaw with RED hair, were wrenched back. He was equally straight-faced.

"I might."

Drew expelled a long breath.

"Relieves me some that you're along. Prophet or priestess, she-devil or woman, this has been brewin' to the point where it's sure enough bustin' loose. I can fair feel the hot breath, right off the fringes of hell."

Chapter Two

Drew's fingers on the reins were at once a command and a caress. The stage swung fast and smoothly through the open gate of the stockade, avoiding a heavily laden wagon on one side and a plodding man on foot on the other. A blue-clad sentry, with no particular regard for military niceties, perched comfortably atop the wide post from which one of the gates was hinged. He cradled a long-barreled, ancient rifle, while his jaws moved in a matching rhythm with Drew's. Another guard watched from the opposite side.

Just inside the compound, in surprising contrast to the weathered hue of the regular buildings, a larger than usual sutler's supply store glistened under a coat of red paint, reminiscent of country barns far to the east. A certain confusion marked the interior of the stockade, where the influx of visitors milled uncertainly.

Drew kicked on the brake, leaning hard on the reins. His glance was disparging.

"We'll eat here," he advised his ravenous load of passengers. "Chew like you'd missed your last dozen meals. I aim to be on our way quicker'n sudden, to make it over the Hump 'fore dark."

The Hump, presumably, lay additional miles to the west. To the uneasiness so apparent to the eyes, evidence accorded the ears was equally unsettling. This was the edge of Comanche country, and there apparently had been isolated outrages, attributed with a ready if unthinking generosity to their account. Certainly the Indians were on the prowl, increasingly restless. There was no telling what might develop. Not all, but many of the settlers from a wide area were scurrying for sanctuary at the post.

Yet not quite all, apparently. An impatient team of broncos, more fitted to the saddle than to run in harness, a stamped and pawed nervously before a section of the long hitching rail which flanked the sutler's store. They were attached to a spring wagon, more fitted to their size than the heavier wagons which had been arriving, laden with all sorts of household goods. By contrast, the buckboard was being stacked with supplies, clearly in preparation for departure.

A cowboy, with legs looking as though

additionally bowed by the weight he carried, big hat tipped askew to the side of his head, came from the store. At his heels was a woman, also laden with groceries, strangely light-stepping and graceful despite their weight. A blue sunbonnet, loosely tied, hung down her back, allowing her hair to show in a soft pile at either side.

Abbott stared, his glance holding, his breath suddenly fast. That hair was a flame, like fire in a forest; not carroty like his own whiskers nor red in any usual sense, not yet auburn. Somehow it was a combination, vivid but not scarlet. Dave Drew caught his glance and jerked his head significantly.

Equally strange were the eyes which, bird-quick, encountered Abbott's and clung, in mutual surprise. Eyes to match the hair, though completely opposite. They were of a sapphire hue, green, on fire with flame of their own. Satan's red-haired squaw!

Almost certainly Drew had been thinking of her when he had used the term, grossly inappropriate though it was. A skin milk-white, which seemed to take no burn from the sun, was in wild contradiction. And yet, at such a time, the stir of trouble like smoke against the sky —

Another man came at her heels, toting a box laden with canned goods. As striking after his own fashion, he was of a matching height with Abbott, bareheaded to the sun. His easy assurance proclaimed him not a clerk but plainly the proprietor, the sutler, Blackjack McQuade.

Amid the surrounding excitement he was as unruffled as the girl.

"Best grade of peaches I've ever been able to get, Miss Shenandoah — ordered them with you in mind." Placing the box on the floor of the buckboard, he tried to take her burden, but she deposited it without help, a rounded arm gleaming whitely smooth as the sleeve fell back.

"But is it wise for you to return to your ranch?" McQuade went on. "Especially in view of everyone else pulling stakes, hustlin' to get here."

"They act like a flock of chickens," Shenandoah returned scornfully. "Someone sees his own shadow, and takes fright and runs, then all the rest follow! They're inviting the very trouble they're afraid of having, leaving everything open and deserted. But even so, I don't believe there will be any."

"Neither do I," the sutler agreed heartily. "Still it worries me, as it always has, you off there with only your housekeeper and a small crew, running a ranch. If anything SHOULD happen — "

"Nothing will, Mr. McQuade," she assured him serenely. Somehow she was magnificent, graceful, doubly surprising, even startling in such a setting. It was more than hair like flame or eyes to rival newsprung grass. Those were symbols. There was a power, almost a strangeness — Abbott thought again of the terms prophetess, priestess, even sorceress —

"Nothing, except that there are chores to do

and I need to be there to do them," she added. "I'll pay you for everything when I get the other load tomorrow. If my credit is good for so long."

"Now was that remark called for?" McQuade protested. "With me, your credit's good for anything, anywhere, any time and well you should know it."

"I've always found cash to be a good builder of credit," Shenandoah returned coolly, and climbed expertly over a wheel to the wagon seat, bending to loosen the reins from about the brake rod. She favored Abbott with a second, appraising, faintly disturbed glance, while the cowboy untied the team, then his own saddled horse. The next moment the restless ponies were off, the girl threading a way as expertly as the jehu among the unusual confusion.

McQuade, about to return to the store, paused as another horseman came, the animal prancing and nervous, a manifest reflection of the mood of its rider. His shoulder bars, along with a more than regulation display of gold braid, proclaimed his rank as being a captain. Like Abbott and McQuade, he was inches taller than most, his hair below the rim of his hat a sun-bleached yellow. The matching mustache accentuated the blueness of nervously darting eyes.

The pony stood, having stopped with bunched hoofs at an ungentle drag on the bridle reins. Abbott sensed that the pair quarreled over the flame-haired woman like dogs over a bone.

The captain was clearly as flustered as any of

the soldiers or visitors who had come crowding, adding to the confusion. For an instant his glance followed the receding back of Shenandoah, firm, assured and serene. From her his eyes took in the stagecoach with its uncertain knot of passengers, sweeping toward Drew, hovering with a touch of doubt on Abbott. Finally they rested accusingly on McQuade.

"That was bad business, Mr. McQuade, to let her go. I credited you with a better judgement, not to say influence!"

McQuade lifted heavy shoulders, then allowed them to drop in a half-mocking shrug. His mouth curved to a smile, but to Abbott, watchfully observant, there was both dislike and contempt.

"Sure now, Captain, you over rate my poor powers of persuasion. Miss O'Shea has a mind of her own, with a will to match. You can't have failed to notice, Mr. Doorley."

Doorley remained staring, big white teeth closing on a frayed strand of mustache. He seemed half-minded to spur after the wagon and attempt to persuade her to remain at the post or even to take stronger action. But already the buckboard was through the gates and trailing a cloud of dust, the cayuses breaking to a run. Doorley swung back to where Drew was giving orders for a fresh team to be readied.

"There will be no hurry as to that," Doorley informed the driver. "No rush at all, in fact. As of now, I am giving orders that the road to the west is closed."

20

Drew bristled, as much from anger as dismay. "Closed?" he repeated. "For what reason?"

"Do you need to ask?" Doorley demanded. "Look at these others. The road, the country around, are unsafe. I'd be negligent of my duties to permit you to proceed."

"Your duties?" Drew's dislike was thinly veiled. Clearly he had clashed with this officer before. "Are those orders from Major Connoly?"

"Major Connoly is a very sick man, and not to be bothered with trifles. I repeat, the road to the west is closed and will remain so for the forseeable future. You see, ah — enjoy our hospitality for the present, along with these others who have seen fit to come in."

Abbott was listening intently. His mind had been half on the red-haired woman, distracted by the name of the Major Connoly! But it was a fairly common name. These sudden orders of Doorley, who was clearly the acting commandant, affected him.

"I have urgent business somewhat further to the west, Captain. Business which admits of no delay."

In Doorley's eyes he thought to detect a flash of malicious satisfaction. Clearly, the captain enjoyed the exercise of authority.

"The road west is closed," Doorley repeated. "For the protection of innocents and fools. Including tenderfeet," he added, with a pointed glance at Abbott's soiled but still fine garments and swung his horse.

Chapter Three

Turning, Abbott met Drew's glance, catching an amused gleam which was replaced by anger.

"The Captain's misjudgment is as hindering as a broken wheel," Drew shrugged. "And the worst part, bad 'cess, is that he seems to have the power to back his orders. As for the stage and myself, with a choice of staying or going — ," he surveyed the disorganized scene grimly. "I'll be toolin' back the way we came, with no waste of time. If you wish to ride alone — "

"Thanks, but I'm afraid not." Abbott was prompt on that point. "My business is out this way."

"It's sorry I am that we can't continue on

together." Drew meant it. "This country has the marks of an unhealthy climate, what with the talk that's been assailin' the ears not only of Wild Horse and his Comanches, but of a great medicine feast and gathering of the peoples — a prophet or messiah called the Bear, sorcerers and magic and what not. But for that I'd circle about and keep on, but Doorley may have a bit of sense in what he says. Thanks for giving me a hand, as you did." He extended a hand.

Abbott gripped it, impressed by Drew's seriousness as well as what was probably a half-fanciful recital. Presently the stagecoach, pulled by fresh horses, its passenger list intact save for himself but swelled by two others, swung out through the gates and turned back toward the red and suddenly ominous glow of sunset.

Abbott eyed it thoughtfully. He could probably obtain a horse and keep on, whether or not that met with Doorley's approval; the lack of it would not concern him too greatly. Once beyond the stockade, which would present no real barrier, he could probably buy a horse from the woman called Shenandoah.

With talk of magic and the threat of war and bloodshed, his thoughts were drawn to her as by a magnet. Hair like flame, or crimson — with contrasting eyes like sapphires and the mein at least of a high priestess if not a goddess!

It was not alone the aura of romance which surrounded her; here there was more and if he'd reached a dead end with the stopping of the stage, there was also a fresh beginning. Indeed, this might be a better starting place than he had expected.

Also there was the Major, obviously a sick man, whose name might or might not be coincidence. Doorley had all but admitted that he was assuming authority which had not been clearly delegated, acting without the knowledge or consent of the commandant, because he was too sick to be bothered — or to interfere — which was in keeping with a power-hungry man, who by chance was in the wrong place at a critical time. Such mistakes occurred. Usually they were merely annoying, but they could result in disaster.

Looking around, it was easy to see that the post was poorly prepared to cope with the emergency which seemed suddenly to have come upon it; though there should have been forewarning enough and to spare. Still, if the commandant was too ill to keep control or perhaps even realize what was going on and Captain Doorley was assuming an authority he was unprepared to handle, the deterioration of affairs became clear.

Soldiers were dashing about, attempting to arrange for the housing of the newcomers, but with something of the frenzy which actuated their captain. Perhaps because of bad orders or the lack of good ones, confusion was mounting rather than being brought under control.

Lacking the Major's oversight, it seemed a fair

judgment that matters were going from bad to worse. An army or a garrison could become inefficient, even demoralized, in a surprisingly short while. Also this post appeared to be short-handed, sadly undermanned, just when real trouble threatened.

But enough newcomers, ranchers and prospectors and trappers were coming in to swell the man-power to a respectable force. Those who sheltered behind the stockade walls should be safe.

But Shenandoah was outside such protection! She had promised to be back the next day for another load of supplies. But it was unlikely that she had any real notion of her own particular risk. It was well to make sure that her ranch was well stocked and she might not be afraid of Indians, and least of all of rumors and wild talk.

Whether she was or not, he and the Captain saw eye to eye as concerned her safety. Abbott was increasingly afraid.

The blast of a bugle, sounding for attention, surprised him along with most others. The gates to the stockade had swung shut.

The soldiers were being marshalled on the only portion of the parade ground still open. They formed in three companies, all of which looked to be well below regulation strength. A lieutenant to each company, but no other captains. Clearly the post was undermanned.

The new arrivals, men and women, even a few children, formed a fourth, loose group, partly out

26

of curiosity but a sergeant was bellowing orders for everyone to assemble.

Abbott's eyes narrowed. He could no longer doubt that the commandant must be very ill. Captain Doorley was more than running wild; he was in danger of running amok.

Doorley galloped his horse around the end of a wagon, forcing a woman and small boy to jump back hastily. Unheeding or even not noticing, Doorley pulled up like a general ready to review his troops. Clearly he relished his moment of glory.

For a dragging minute he stared at the gathering and a hush succeeded the stir. The soldiers were orderly, and the newcomers were curious or impressed. Only a young child cried fearfully.

"Attention!" Doorley shouted. "Now don't be alarmed," he went on, his manner intimidating. "You've all come here to escape the Indians, so you're safe enough. We're going to make sure of that. I intend to take proper precautions, certain necessary steps."

He fell silent, his glance forbidding under heavy brows — an effect he neither understood nor intended, Abbott decided. The new arrivals waited between expectancy and a growing apprehension. The realization that the man in charge was unsure of himself did not make for confidence.

"All this comes at a bad time," Doorley went on. "Bad for us because Major Connoly is temporarily indisposed. It is also difficult because needed reinforcements have been unwarrantably slow in arriving. That finds us short-handed, well below strength."

Again he subjected them to silence. Faces paled, feet shuffled. After the manner of a hell-fire and brimstone evangelist, he was painting a picture in bleak terms. Whether he could offer salvation at the end seemed unlikely.

"That is the situation." His tone was sepeulchral. "And I scarcely need to remind you of what you've been telling me, that we may be called upon to fight for our very lives. We are faced with a grave emergency, one which affects us all."

Once more, while they looked back in growing apprehension, he stared unwinkingly, then barked suddenly.

"Faced with so desperate a situation, I am proclaiming a state of emergency. Everyone is included in its provisions. Every ablebodied man, not already in uniform, I am inducting into the armed forces of the United States, for the duration of this emergency."

His smile was obviously intended to be reassuring. After such a pronouncement, it was a ghastly travesty.

"In that way, the depleted ranks of our forces will be in some measure restored to adequate strength, and more important, everyone will be under proper discipline, and so able to render the best possible service. A service required of all. Mr.

DeKalb, Mr. Jennings, Mr. Van Dyke, you will proceed immediately to register every newcomer, even the names of women and children. Then you will issue uniforms and equipment to the men, assigning the new recruits equally and impartially among your companies."

His glance was coldly intimidating. The fugitives stared back, between shock and disbelief. Such action was as high-handed as it was unexpected.

A brawny farmer stepped forward, clearly minded to protest. Doorley instantly bawled an order.

"Corporal Mehagan! Take charge of that man! Lieutenants, you have your orders."

He was away in a thunder of hoofs. Whatever else might be said of him, Captain Doorley had a sense for the dramatic.

Chapter Four

There was angry protest from many of the men and some of the women, who had looked upon themselves as guests at the fort and under its protection. Doorley's conduct was high-handed but there was not much that anyone could do about it. The soldiers were in the majority and they obeyed orders, listening for the most part with respect and good nature to a venting of anger. That subsided as most realized that as a temporary expedient the action might be helpful. The very number of those seeking sanctuary convinced everyone that this might be more than just a scare.

Abbott listened with a matching amazement,

then he shrugged. He was prepared to stick around this part of the country until the situation developed and clarified. So this new device would not greatly matter. It might even work advantageously.

Any attempt to slip away was being sharply guarded against. Abbott remained with the unexpected recruits, while the officers prepared for the enrollment. Lieutenant DeKalb, square-faced and solemn, prepared to transcribe names to a record book. He surveyed the assembled group, then, at the resentment in nearly every face, an unlooked-for twinkle shone in his eyes.

"Ladies and gentlemen, I understand at least a little of your surprise and how you feel. But the measure is intended for the common good, the protection of all. Also, gentlemen, if this lasts very long, there is the possibility that you'll be paid for your time, instead of doing much the same thing, for nothing. Mind you, that's merely given as an opinion, not a promise, but still a likelihood."

Such a prospect helped mollify the dissenters. His proffer of a rattle to a weeping child drew lifted eyebrows from the mother, but at the little girl's obvious delight she voiced no protest. Abbott recognized the rattle as dried finger bones, which DeKalb had picked up somewhere. Whether or not he realized that it had been a cherished possession of some brave, a noise-maker and medicine piece for war or ceremonial dances,

DeKalb gave no sign.

"Now, if you'll give me your names — " he added, and opened the journal.

He repeated each one, writing in a clerkly hand. William M. Abbott came near the middle of the list, and caused no flutter of interest. Lacking orders, DeKalb also lacked the imagination to inquire into the background of any of them, even as to whether or not they had ever served with the armed forces. That ommission was somewhat remedied in Abbott's case as, issued a uniform from the surplus stocks at the sutler's store, he was assigned to the newly strengthened C Company, along with other additions.

Sergeant Young, whose graying and thinning thatch belied his name, surveyed them disparagingly. Then, with practiced eye, he looked closer at Abbott, suddenly barking a question.

"Abbott! You've worn the uniform before?"

Abbott nodded. "I have."

"A soldier has a look about him," Young explained for the benefit of the others. "And we've few enough soldiers here — old or new." He took an immediate decision. "C Company is short a corporal. You'll serve as acting corporal, beginning now."

With the last light fading, not much could be done that day beyond issuing uniforms and assigning to companies. Doorley seemed to feel that he had done all that was possible, leaving it to the others to implement what he had decreed.

For the moment, there was no opportunity for

personal concerns, and a direct question about the commandant would almost certainly be misunderstood. Another man came riding out of the dusk, astride a lathered horse. His report did nothing to alleviate the increasing apprehension.

"I came across a couple of dead men, off by Wagner Gulch. Poor devils had lost their hair. Since from the way the flies were swarmin', it couldn' have been long before, I didn't hang around."

This was the first tangible report of real trouble, and it was ominous. Until then, there had been unrest and threat, but nothing beyond rumor. Of that, as Abbott could have testified, there was an overabundance, even a thousand miles to the East

It appeared that a party of young braves, eager to demonstrate to more cautious elders how whites should be dealt with, had taken matters into their own hands. The man who made the report estimated a dozen ponies had been in the bunch.

Cooler heads on both sides had hoped to avoid such an outbreak. Now that it had happened, serious trouble was all but inevitable.

Abbott had exchanged a few words with Swan, a rancher at once cool-headed and knowledgeable. He questioned him now.

"What do you figure has stirred the 'Manches to such a pitch?"

"A lot of things." Swan's shrug was eloquent of disgust. "Trouble's been building quite a while, not too bad to start with but allowed to get worse, 'stead of being controlled by the army, which is their job. A month back it could have been managed without much difficulty. Even a week ago, with a firm stand. Only it wasn't done. I reckon the trouble was that the Major has just been too sick to manage."

"And Doorley's pretty much in charge, instead?"

"And that's the main trouble, hereabouts at least. There's reports of a sort of confederation of tribes, but that's a long way from here. I'll give Cap'n Doorley credit for realizin' that something needed to be done, and he set out to try. But he went at it like startin' a fire with coal oil. You throw a can full on a flame, and the next thing, your house is gone."

"What did he do, particularly?"

"Well, the one that blew the lid off was when a few bucks drove off a bunch of horses. Doorley took out after them — and had the bad luck to catch up. Or he thought he did."

"You mean he found the wrong bunch?"

"Yes and no. From the way I heard it, Wild Horse was as bad upset as Doorley, when he heard about it. Wild Horse has been trying to keep his bucks under control. He didn't lose any time in catchin' up with the thieves, and he made them head back with the animals they'd swiped, intending to return them. Maybe even with an apology, though I wouldn't know about that.

"But as bad luck would have it, Doorley

happened along right about then, and instead of lookin' the ground over, he barged in and accused Wild Horse of stealing the horses. Havin' twice as many men as the Indians, and the drop, he ordered Wild Horse whipped, which was an even worse mistake. And THEN he made it worse by turning him loose."

Swan's estimate was only too accurate. Doorley had set out to make an example of the trouble-makers, but he had made all the wrong moves. Chief Wild Horse, from being at least a nominal friend, had been transformed into an enemy.

A few careful questions regarding the commandant elicited even more cautious responses. The men were clearly fearful of saying much. But it was clear that the Major had been a very sick man over a period of many weeks, too ill to realize what was happening or concern himself with the running of the post.

"He's had a high fever, been out of his head a lot of the time," One man admitted. "The Lieutenants have done what they could, looking after him, and from what I hear, he's some better the last day or two. But he's sure been sick."

Incomplete as was the account, it seemed clear that Connoly had been stricken with a serious illness, from which it was almost a miracle that he had survived.

"But what about the doctor? Or is the fort without one?" Abbott asked, making a shrewd guess at the truth.

36

"That's it, we don't have no medico. Not since spring. Doc Henry was a good man, only his horse fell on him just about the time the Major was took sick. I suppose likely the Cap'n sent out word, askin' for a replacement, but nobody's been sent. Not yet, anyway."

That explained much which had seemed incomprehensible. A man out of his head with fever, and too weak to act even if he had had an inkling of what was going on, could not be blamed for neglect of duty.

The three lieutenants impressed Abbott as competent officers, but Captain Doorley clearly had not consulted with them, or if so, had made his own decisions, which they had been helpless to counter. Apparently Doorley had been too busy to more than occasionally look in on the Major. That the lieutenants had looked after the commandant as well as possible indicated both their loyalty to him and the desperation with which they had hoped for his early recovery.

Meanwhile, flushed with authority and delusions of his own importance, Doorley had succeeded only in demonstrating his incompetence and making wrong moves. A combination of events had played into his hands.

Abbott was thoughtful as he watched stars stake out patterns overhead. With luck, it might be that Connoly would regain his strength and ability to command before too long. The difficulty was that, having been so ill for so long, he would not be physically strong enough to do

37

much for days or weeks. And the crisis would wait.

Self-seekers had made hay while they had the chance. Captain Doorley's motives had probably been good, but there was a vast difference between good intentions and good performance. Others had taken advantage.

If he could look in on Connoly, judge for himself, perhaps manage a few words — it was a risky business, but he was not likely to be granted permission or given an interview, and there was no time to waste. And he'd taken chances of greater magnitude, though perhaps for stakes no higher.

And while he was about it, there were other matters, perhaps of equal importance. The freight wagon which had been in trouble with a broken wheel had come in just ahead of darkness, sliding well enough on the pole in place of the wheel. With the pole for a marker, Abbott had no difficulty in identifying it, drawn up alongside the side doors to the sutler's big building. Surprisingly, along with the other two wagons, it had already been unloaded.

A heavy hasp was in place, the doors padlocked shut.

In such troublous times, that might be a sensible precaution, but it was surprising, since the store was inside the stockade, rather than beyond. And that too, was somewhat unusual. The usual custom was for the sutler to build outside.

Had it been beyond the walls, locked doors would be a necessity. But inside — either McQuade was inordinately careful, or he might have reasons for such conduct.

The windows to the store were as tightly shut, secured from the inside.

Abbott was blinking thoughtfully at the star pattern when a revolver barrel jabbed hard against his stomach. In the half-light behind it he made out McQuade, teeth as prominent as in his genial smile of earlier in the day, only this time forming an intimidating snarl.

"And what might you be about, my bucko?" he demanded. "What's the meaning of this prowling? Talk fast, before I let daylight in at one side of you and out the other!"

Chapter Five

Abbott's judgement of the sutler was confirmed. A surface geniality was no more than a cloak for viciousness. And he and Doorley, clearly, were rivals for Shenandoah's favor! Between them they held most of the power at the post, including life or death. No wonder she had been ready to risk the Indians in preference.

"I know you," McQuade went on. "You're that tenderfoot from the stage, and it's mistrustful I am of all such as a matter of principle. Speak quick!"

"I was doing the same as yourself," Abbott shrugged. "Checking to make sure that all was well, in the process having a look by your store.

Conditions being as they are, it was deemed a sensible precaution."

"With that I agree. But whose idea was this, to give you such authority, or the right to prowl?"

Abbott's answer was prompt. "Sergeant Young. On his authority, I'm now acting corporal of Charley Company."

That was true, and a reasonable bluff. Should McQuade go to Young for confirmation, Abbott was sure that the sergeant would back him.

Still uncertain, McQuade holstered his revolver.

"Great minds run in the same channels." He could not resist a gibe. "And sometimes lesser ones. Good night to you — Corporal."

His attitude pretty well confirmed Abbott's suspicion, formed back at the canyon where the wagon wheel had cracked under strain. For one reason, the load was considerably heavier than the manifest of goods indicated. Almost certainly the sutler was taking advantage of his position as a civilian, while working with and almost within the army, to add to his nominal profits. Those heavy crates almost surely contained guns, not harnesses. Rifles brought in despite regulations, under the nose of the army, with its protection.

By now of course they had been unloaded, and were safely stored inside the big warehouse, held under lock and key. McQuade's key.

Under circumstances which prevailed, starting to come to a head after long ferment, such guns were logical; they even helped explain the concurrent build-up. This would in all likelihood

42

be the final shipment of guns, a sizeable supply accumulated at the store, to be turned over to the Comanches on the eve of war . . . An eve now at hand, as was the red dawn to follow.

In his dual position, McQuade could fill such customers' needs at little risk but a big profit. Nor would this be the first time that a sutler had misused his position.

Abbott paid Captain Doorley the doubtful compliment of ignorance as to what was going on. Others might harbor suspicions, but they were not in a position to act. It had been a perfect set-up, and McQuade had taken advantage.

Obtaining proof would be another matter. Suspicious of Abbott's prowling, he would be doubly careful, but with warfare imminent, he could hardly draw back from so dangerous a game, even with a change of heart. But any change would be of the head, not the heart. Renegades who misused their position to supply guns to the enemy had long since smothered all remnants of conscience.

Even if he wanted to draw back, McQuade was probably too deeply involved to permit any change of mind. The only difference might be a need to alter plans for delivery.

Abbott's problem was how to make use of what he suspected, lacking proof. Power at the post was concentrated in the hands of Doorley and McQuade. They could be ruthless in its application, and both had come to regard him

43

with suspicion, heightened by dislike.

"Sure and't is not only the sinful who stand in slippery places," Abbott thought ruefully. "Or belike I'm being too kind to myself. But it's watch your step or be upended!"

Whatever his motives, Captain Doorley, a decision taken, lost no time in implementing it. Sun-up found the post astir, officers and non-coms at work with their still surprised, half-bewildered recruits. As the sun sweated toward its crest, Abbott had the assurance that, if he had a pair of enemies at the post, he also had made a few friends.

Lieutenant Jennings and Sergeant Young, anxious to improve C Company to the fullest possible extent, worked to assimilate the newcomers, to fit them into the pattern. They had redoubled reason, of which the increasing threat was only a part. When Captain Doorley rode on a scout, as he had a way of doing without warning and often without reason, always he picked Charley Company as escort.

In this process of assimilating the new men, they were finding Abbott invaluable. He worked hard, requiring no orders from his superiors, which both realized they would at times be unready to supply. He showed no hesitation. Clearly, he had done this sort of thing before. Soldiering, to him, had been a habit, laid awhile aside, resumed again as readily as he had donned the uniform.

With noon approaching, Young called a halt, not alone to rest tired men but to allow himself a breather.

"At ease," he bawled, and, catching his Lieutenant's eye, permitted himself the ghost of a smile. Companies F and A, which might not too inaptly be labeled Frantic and Awful, had worked as hard but to manifestly less purpose. Officers and non-coms alike had succeeded mostly in confusing everyone, themselves included. Captain Doorley had observed for a while from a distance, but he had not interfered or offered any suggestions.

Though it was not a notion to be voiced, the thought was in the minds of ranks and officers alike, that Doorley had refrained, not from courtesy, but simply because he discerned nothing wrong. The captain's aptitudes had long since been privately discussed.

"Strikes me that it's a case of a throw-back, like in the European armies of a century or so ago," a scholarly private had explained it. "In those days the army was a career. The second sons of an earl or maybe a duke, bought an officer's commission in the army or navy. Being a lord or viscount was supposed to be all that was necessary to make a man a good officer. If some poor devils got killed because he wasn't — well, that was too bad, but it didn't much matter.

"Now, a man's supposed to have some ability, to get promoted, up to as far as a captain. But mistakes happen." He had let it go at that.

45

The lieutenant and the sergeant were long-time friends. Each respected the other; not only had they campaigned together, but they had saved each others' lives. Jennings confided something of what was in his mind.

"He's been an officer. I'd give you odds on that. There's something about the way he speaks. Just his tone carries command. And whatever else he is, he's no tenderfoot."

Young added his own accolade.

"Charley Company's mighty lucky."

A measure of order was being restored to the overcrowded space inside the walls. Today the big gates remained closed, having had no occasion to open, until an approaching trail of dust resolved itself into a team of racing broncos, jerking along the empty spring wagon. Today, Shenandoah rode with sunbonnet tied at chin but thrown back, disclosing the ripe flame of her hair. Even without that, Abbott would have had no difficulty in recognizing the trim, erect figure on the seat, handling reins and horses with easy skill.

The same cowboy accompanied her as on the day before, riding alongside. Today there was one difference. A saddle-sheath had been added, and in it was stacked a Sharp's.

Appraised of their approach, Captain Doorley gave orders for the gates to be set wide. Together with McQuade, rushing not to be outdone, they formed a welcoming committee as the wagon swept through, on and past to McQuade's store.

They were alongside at the sudden stop, and the Captain doffed his hat in a sweeping gesture.

"It's a relief to all of us that nothing untoward has happened," he concluded a flowery welcome. "I've been angry with myself for allowing you to take such chances, Miss O'Shea."

"Allow?" Shenandoah repeated, and her eyelashes seemed to take fire from the hair above. "I have a ranch, a home, and I go and come as I please." In virtual dismissal, she turned to McQuade. "I want another load of goods."

McQuade, still in the saddle, managed to outreach the depth of Doorley's bow. His eyes, sweeping his rival, held a hint of malice.

"Of course, Miss Shenandoah, of course. And I'm sure a lady such as yourself runs no great risk. You'll want help in loading." Glancing around, his eyes fixed on Abbott. He beckoned blandly.

"You'll require a soldier to assist. I'm sure the Captain is agreeable."

Doorley looked annoyed, but he was quick to dissemble.

"By all means. Give Miss O'Shea a hand, Soldier."

His face expressionless, Abbott followed Shenandoah. So milk-white a throat below the flame of hair, the saucily proud tilt to nose and shin was both entrancing and disturbing. Such a woman was not merely a rarity here on the frontier; here, like anywhere was not often to be met with.

She wore no perfume, as her sisters farther to the east might have done, but there was an emanation, a freshness equally pleasing. With clearly mischievious intent she had surveyed him, then extended a hand for assistance in alighting, smiling with cool amusement at the surprised, almost shocked looks on the faces of Doorley and McQuade.

Beyond voicing instructions she ignored him in turn. Abbott loaded out supplies as McQuade filled her orders.

The sutler ran a well-stocked store, making use of every foot of space. Goods were stacked high along both sides of narrow aisles, leading to shadowy recesses. Abbott's eyes were busy. In contrast to the confused conditions at the post, due to the long illness of its commandant, the store was carefully ordered. It was apparent that McQuade gave at least as much consideration to the needs of the settlers as the requirements of the army; which was not quite orthodox but almost certainly profitable.

Irregularities had become increasingly common during the war, many persisting in its backwash. This post was isolated, and without an active commandant to prod a distant headquarters, for the time it seemed virtually forgotten. Doorley and McQuade had taken advantage of the opportunity, each in his own way.

Shenandoah had a considerable list of goods in mind. She gave them like a sergeant rattling orders, setting a couple of clerks scurrying along with McQuade. Finally she paused for a more leisurely survey, considering what was available, weighing it against need or desire. The wagon was all but loaded.

Abbott found leisure to drift unobserved among the high-piled supplies, which toward the back of the store formed an aisle so shadowy as to be almost a cavern.

His glance quickened. Here was what he had looked for, not a single case as he'd hefted the day before, but several crates, all alike. Rifles, almost certainly, along with ammunition. These would not be the regulation guns, issued to the men on duty.

His hunch was that these weapons would be far more modern, more devastating in battle. Some might already have been supplied to the Indians, encouraging them in the course they were taking. Equipped with the number stocked here, even trained militiamen and with companies at full strength, would be a poor match for the hosts being marshalled against them.

Abbott pondered. As an outsider, interference on his part would be sharply resented. But he was in it, partly because of Doorley's high-handedness. That he was increasingly interested and concerned for Shenandoah might be irrelevant, but also vital.

The things he had come to suspect were serious enough, amounting in his mind to conviction. But proof was something else, and without that, to prefer charges which he might not be able to substantiate could be disastrous; not merely for himself, but for everyone at the post — or beyond its gates.

With the wagon box piled high, Shenandoah was ready to return to her ranch. On that point at least, Abbott found himself in agreement with Captain Doorley. He didn't like it.

During the loading, Doorley had been called away. Now he was back, clearly wrestling with the same dilemma as bothered Abbott. With mounting excitement he expressed his opposition to Shenandoah either returning to or remaining at the ranch.

"Trouble with the Indians is no longer a mere possibility," he pointed out. "Men have been killed, and that will lead to more clashes. At the ranch, you would be defenseless. Surely, ma'am, you can see how much better it is for you to remain here, to make use of the facilities, the hospitality which we are prepared to extend, at least until the situation improves."

"Hospitality! Army style?" Her short laugh brought a flush to his cheeks.

"I have endeavored to act for the common good," Doorley reminded her stiffly. "But it would be additionally — even personally distressing to me, should anything happen to you."

Standing near the hitch-rail, Abbott obeyed Shenandoah's signal to untie the team. This time unassisted, she climbed quickly to the wagon seat, gathering up the reins.

"I appreciate your concern, Captain, but I have a ranch to look after. I can't afford to allow it to be destroyed, at least not without making an effort to preserve it. I have a good crew, and I'm sure we'll manage. Of course — ."

Abbott was certain that she spoke on impulse, solely to tantalize Doorley. Her eyes fixed on him.

"Of course, if you should care to send a soldier to aid, such as this man, I might not refuse."

Doorley was taken aback. Anger, a touch of jealousy, grated in his voice.

"I'm afraid that is out of the question. Abbott is acting corporal of C Company. Some one else — "

"I wouldn't care for anyone else. So, if I must go without him, I'll make sure of getting back well before dark."

This was more than rebuff. Doorley reddened angrily.

"You will observe, Miss O'Shea, that the gates are closed. They will remain so. I have issued orders that no one — no one — is to be allowed to depart."

Shenandoah's face flamed in turn. She leaned toward him, clutching the horsewhip.

"Captain Doorley, you are insufferable. You have acted high-handedly with others, but I am a civilian, and not a man, and in no way subject to your orders or jurisdiction. You will have that gate reopened at once, or I will horsewhip you as you deserve!"

Doorley hesitated, appalled. He knew that she would do exactly as she threatened. He could back away, or issue orders for others to grab her, but either course would be undignified, moreover he was far from sure that he would be obeyed. Or he could snatch for the whip, engaging in an unseemly brawl with a woman. Each possibility was unthinkable.

McQuade, a sardonic smile touching the edges of his mouth, came to his rescue.

"Sure now, Captain, and it runs in my mind that the lady knows what she is about, that the danger is none so great. In case of attack, a flag hoisted, or other signal, can bring a party from here in rescue, and the place is like a fortress, so it is."

It was a way out, however humiliating. The bitter conviction that his own hopes as a suitor for this lady's hand had been irreparably ruined, while those of the smugly smiling sutler were enhanced, flamed from jealousy to hate. But Doorley maintained a dignity of sorts. He lifted his hat, stepping back.

"I had intended no interference, only your welfare. Since this is your decision — "

He signaled the sentry at the gate, swung sharply, and marched away with such dignity as he could muster.

Chapter Six

Major John Connoly became aware of the sun, stealing in at his window, not as an intolerable brightness against fever-weakened eyes, or for enervating heat atop the burn of fever, but as a friendly substance once liked but almost forgotten. With it, through the open window, came the distant song of a meadowlark, the notes sweet as a spill of silver, from beyond the stockade. He listened with a sense of awareness, of pleasure as opposed to sickness akin to nightmare.

A brass bell with handle was on the stand alongside the bed. Aware of a growing sense of hunger, he reached for the bell, shaking it, bewildered to find even so small an effort taxing to his strength. Replacing the bell, his fingers strayed to his face, and at the ragged growth of beard, the gauntness of sunken cheeks, he lay a while, appalled and confused.

Then an orderly entered, saluting, his freckled face breaking into a sudden grin as he saw that his commandant was taking an interest, for the first time in weeks.

"Yes sir, Major?" The words were formal, but Connoly detected the pleasure in the tones.

"I'm hungry, Grayson — starved! Bring me breakfast — dinner — " He considered the idea with growing favor. "Supper too, while you're about it. A beefsteak to start with — "

"Yes SIR! Something to eat. I'll pass the word immediately, sir."

Within a surprisingly short while he was back, bearing a tray on which a small bowl of soup reposed, its rising steam redolent of beef. In substance it was tantalizing, but thin. Even with a few morsels of bread immersed, it did no better than whet the edge of a suddenly ravenous appetite. The Major scraped the bottom of the bowl, then looked up impatiently.

"That was all right for a starter," he conceded. "But isn't my steak ready by now?"

"Begging the Major's pardon, sir, but Mr. Jennings says that's all for the present. He'll be along to see you as soon as possible — within a short time — "

"All?" Connoly exploded. "Jennings? Who

gives orders here, him or me? I want a steak — with potatoes and gravy and coffee and pie."

The providential arrival of Lieutenant Jennings enabled the flustered orderly to retreat. Expressing his warm pleasure at finding the Major so much improved, Jennings explained, as tactfully as possible, how very sick Connoly had been, how they had feared for his life and that it was the unanimous opinion of everyone that it would be a serious, even a fatal mistake, to overdo at the table with returning appetite, however promising such hunger was.

Disgruntled but forced to agree, Connoly questioned him as to what had happened during his period of illness, an interval in time of which he had only the haziest of recollections. He received a sketchy and incomplete fill-in, along with the present worsening state of affairs. His waning attention, shortened by fatigue, was spurred by the disclosure that the possible but remote threat of Indian trouble had become a reality. But he was nodding, too weak to concentrate, falling back, almost instantly asleep.

Awakening a few hours later, doubly ravenous and strengthened by a bigger dish of soup, he was given more details. They were far from complete, but enough to leave him dismayed at his weakness, and appalled by reports of Doorley's ineptitude and headlong course with the settlers who had sought refuge.

Lieutenant Jennings had been careful to volunteer no opinion, but he had answered questions honestly. Connoly lay back after he had gone, resisting the impulse to send at once for Doorley, trying to fit the pieces in to place, to adjust to what he had learned. Since he had been incapacitated at a critical time and unable to command, Doorley could hardly be censured for taking charge.

He must have a fuller knowledge of the situation, a fair evaluation, before issuing his own orders. It would be foolish to follow Doorley's example and be wild and headlong, before he understood the implications.

Ringing for Grayson, he instructed the orderly to bring him the list of names of the newly inducted recruits. He was acquainted with many who would be on it.

The roster was surprisingly long, which in itself was revealing. Clearly the situation had worsened beyond what Jennings had revealed or he had suspected, with so many settlers from so wide a territory flocking in; that most of them, ruggedly independent, would probably have stayed out and taken their chances with the Indians, rather than to come under military authority, Connoly had not the slightest doubt. But Doorley had sprung his trap after they were within its jaws.

He had overstepped his authority, and would have to be disciplined. But with the situation so dangerously close to getting out of hand, the Major wanted to know the background, to be sure of himself before he acted.

Questioned as to the list, Grayson's replies

added to his bafflement as much as they enlightened. Propped with pillows, Connoly struggled through the lists, dismayed again at his own weakness, how swiftly he tired.

All three lieutenants had been trapped by discipline and regulations, but none had shown such initiative as clearly should have been exercised. Doorley's had been the only strong hand, and to gallop headlong in the wrong direction was hardly helpful —

Connoly straightened with sudden interest. These were the men who had been added to C Company, and one name seemed to leap out. On the verge of sinking tiredly back, he was suddenly wide awake. Forgetting the bell, he bellowed with increasing volume for the orderly.

"Here!" His finger was on the line, pointing it out. "Bring me this new recruit, Abbott. William Montana Abbott. Never mind what he's doing. I want him here, on the double."

Chapter Seven

Success, like strong liquor, is a heady draught. One drink creates a taste for more. To that rule, the sutler was no exception. In every aspect or venture save one, since assuming his duties as the store-keeper, things had gone well for Blackjack McQuade. The set-back he had received could be— would be — no more than temporary. Since it concerned so self-sufficient but beautiful a woman as Shenandoah O'Shea, it was a whet to the appetite.

Shenandoah would have been surprised could she gave guessed that McQuade had mapped out his future at his first sight of her, some years before. By some alchemy of its own, that glimpse had transformed him from an easy-going near-loafer to a man of driving ambition. The prospects, as he envisioned them, were dazzling — wealth and position, respect and power. They would become possible with so lovely a wife, transforming everything. Not only could she supply those niceties in which he was lacking but beauty and ability, teamed with his, must carry him far.

Certain obstacles had presented themselves. An annoying but not very worrisome one was Captain Doorley, who just as clearly had been smitten by her charms, and who accounted himself a ladies' man. But he could be dealt with, and time had convinced McQuade that Doorley posed no real problem.

The greatest obstacle was himself — his reputation as Blackjack McQuade, notorious for ruthlessness across half a dozen territories. Until then he had taken pride in his toughness, but in the new vision it was a handicap. He had taken the first step by setting up as a merchant, enabled to step into the post upon his predecessor's sudden decision to quit. That McQuade had provided potent reasons for the other man to step down had gone unrealized by most.

The disparity of age between Shenandoah and himself had been no worry. He felt young, and looked well under his years. He had set about his courtship assiduously.

To be rebuffed at every turn had puzzled, then

angered him, but it had served to increase his determination. No one stood long in his way. Those who tried learned a bitter lesson.

Watching Shenandoah head away from the fort, he was as pleased by the turn of events as Doorley was disgruntled. Luck was playing into his hands. Whether she believed it or not, trouble was on the way, big trouble. She would be forced to turn to him for protection, since he was the one man who could provide it.

"And if, like a fractious young filly, she still needs a touch of the whip, I'll know how to provide that, too," he mused. A sudden notion, daring as it was dazzling, had struck him, with heretofore unguessed possibilities. He berated himself that it had been so slow in coming; still from all reports he was not too late, but providentially timed.

"With the White Bear looking not only for a sign, but for a red-haired, green-eyed sorceress — and if I provde her — "

It would be a chancy business, high with risk, but again he saw the possibilities of more power, a widening influence along the path he had already chosen, however temporarily. Certainly it should provide the touch of the gad.

Night had fallen. The compound was quieter, orderly, as the influx of visitors accomodated themselves to altered conditions. The stars hung wide and bright, a sprinkle of pale gold against the canopy in which they were outspread. McQuade eyed them appreciatively. It required no stretching of the imagination to believe that they twinkled. One, in particular, low against the horizon, compounded the illusion.

Having expected such a signal, he had prepared. He approached the sentry at the closed gates, his coming heralded by the rich smoke of a costly cigar. Puffing at it contentedly, it glowed in miniature emulation of the other points of light.

"Is that you, Mister McQuade?" The sentry was respectful. "I recognized your cigar," he added. "It has a fragrance all its own."

"Why, so it does, and so it should," McQuade conceded. "I import them especially for my own use." He chuckled quietly. "I laid in an extra supply, with the Major in mind, but with the poor man too ill even to think of a smoke, they are by way of becoming stale. But one man's bad luck can be another's fortune. Since you like them, have several." He thrust a handful upon the astonished sentry.

"Why — why — for me, sir? I — I can't begin to thank you — "

"Don't try. They'd only go to waste, which would be a pity. And when you enjoy them, why, here's a bit of a bottle to add to the pleasure." Poor as was the light, the closing of one eye did not escape the sentry. He accepted the pint flask with alacrity.

"You're a gentleman, sir. A gentleman and a — a scholar." His tongue hesitated over such unfamiliar phraseology, but his appreciation was evident.

"Think nothing of it." McQuade was expansive. "I've stood such a shift in my own time and know how tiring it becomes, also the chill once the sun is well gone. That wind from the west blows cold. So I'll be seeking my own warm blankets."

He strolled away, his path marked by the drifting smoke, then ducked suddenly behind a wagon. As he had counted on, the wait was brief. Having planted the suggestion, knowing the weakness of the man on watch, he was not surprised when, having sniffed the bottle, the sentry, with sudden decision, set his teeth to the cork and wrenched it loose with a twist of head and jaws. The wind WAS cold.

Not too much later, protected now from the push of the wind in a sheltered nook, the level of the flask was being steadily lowered. The guard would be in for a reprimand the next day, perhaps a stay in the guard house, but he would count it as worth it. Unhurriedly, unnoticed, McQuade let himself out. He kept to the deeper shadows of the stockade wall for some distance, branching away where a clump of cottonwoods and willows followed a small watercourse. In their comfortable shelter he was not surprised to find Chief Wild Horse awaiting him.

"I saw your signal," McQuade confirmed. "I was expecting it."

The chief was an outstanding specimen of red man, tall and powerful, proud alike of his race and position. McQuade knew something of his history, having been more than a little surprised, at their first meeting some years before, a gathering of cattlemen and prospectors, of merchants, army officers and a smattering of politicians, to discover an Indian among so overwhelming a concourse of whites. Not only that, but as well and matchingly dressed, conversing on an equal footing with the leaders of frontier life.

McQuade had not been surprised when one of the number had mentioned that Wild Horse had received an education at a white man's school.

He had been startled upon finding that Wild Horse, like himself, was a member of an ancient and honored fraternity, dating back to almost nameless antiquity. McQuade had all but forgotten the order or its rites, or his one-time participation.

Some day, when his dreams were fulfilled, it might be profitable to remember.

Wild Horse was a man of parts; that he had won his leadership more than other chiefs was not surprising.

Their acquaintance had developed, though never to the point of friendship. Each saw in the other possibilities, and had reacted accordingly. This meeting had been arranged well in advance.

That Wild Horse held all white men in contempt and with a bitter hatred, McQuade was aware; that he had remained until very recently a voice of moderation the sutler understood as well. Wild Horse was too long-sighted a leader to rush headlong into disaster, to lead his people foolishly even when they clamored to be taken to war. But the senseless slaughter of trusting men had infuriated him.

McQuade was under no illusions, and that had been the case from the start. His vision and planning, though from a different point of view, were as long as Wild Horse's.

Wild Horse wasted no words. "You have the guns?"

McQuade nodded. They were too distant from the walls of the stockade for their voices to carry.

"They came in last night."

"About time. I want them, now."

"And you'll get them," McQuade assured him. "But not tonight. There are difficulties." He did not insult his confederate's intelligence by elaborating. "A diversion must first be created."

"Of what nature?"

"One which you will find profitable. Also it should be to the liking of those of your warriors who grow restless. You know the ranch of the lady called O'Shea?"

"She of the hair like a flame?" Wild Horse was clearly startled.

"Yes."

It was never necessary with this man to draw a map or elaborate on a plan. Like a lead wolf, his mind outraced the pack, to cut ahead for a flanking attack.

"You would raid her herd?" Wild Horse was still surprised.

McQuade saw the necessity to explain.

"I've been sweet on the lady for some time, and am still. But for her own good she needs a lesson. Once you really unloose your braves, some will be difficult to restrain. For her to remain at the ranch, as she is determined to do, could mean her death. I would not have that."

Wild Horse nodded his comprehension.

"We run off her herd — creating the diversion you require. After which there will be no reason for her to remain out there to look after them."

"Tomorrow night," McQuade confirmed. "I will attend to my part. Only I must have your assurance for her safety."

The chief's reply was faintly puzzling.

"Wild Horse wars on white men. Not on women. In any case, everyone would make very sure that she comes to no harm."

The meeting was concluded, but not quite as McQuade had planned. There came the muffled thud of unshod hoofs, then a running horse came sweeping across the misty open, on into the shadows — an Indian pony, ridden arrogantly by a brave with the taste of victory on his tongue.

He pulled up, the hoofs of his hard-driven animal sliding in the soft turf. His glance slanted with contemptuous recognition at McQuade, but it was to the chief that he addressed himself. The words, in native dialect, were meaningless to the sutler. But a ray of the rising moon penetrated through an opening in the leafy canopy overhead, picking out the adornment of the warrior, tied at a fringe of the thong which served him in lieu of a belt.

They were a pair of scalps. One was black-haired, the other, long and silkily golden, had come unmistakably from the head of a woman. McQuade felt a little sick.

Chapter Eight

No string of singing wires spanned these still all but untenanted runs of the border, but even with such a lack, news had a way of running, of outracing the fastest pony. How it managed was often a mystery, even to the old timers, but that it did the knowledgeable had long since accepted. Some had termed the process, and accurately enough, a moccasin telegraph.

Whatever or however, the report was on everyone's tongue with the rise of the sun, of fresh atrocities committed not distant from the fort, added and unmistakable proof that trouble was no longer merely imminent but at hand. Captain Doorley took note, and determined action.

"They leave us little choice," he confided to his lieutenants. "These red devils must be taught a lesson, and at once. Otherwise the whole affair is in danger of getting out of hand."

At such a time, the Major would have requested the views of his officers, have considered them fairly and perhaps discussed them. Only after so sensible a precaution and proper courtesy would he have acted. Doorley, as usual, ommitted both. He issued his orders.

"Prepare your company, Mr. Jennings. Each man with ten rounds of ammunition. We will move within the hour."

The pronoun made clear that, as usual, he would head the expedition. That an acting commandant might do better to remain at the fort, allowing the lieutenant to take responsibility, either did not occur to him or was put aside. Doorley was not one to designate even a minor command to others. And, again as usual, he forgot or neglected to name one of the two remaining officers of equal rank to the seniority of command while he was gone.

Catching the look on Jennings' face, DeKalb grinned wryly.

"You have my sympathy. Even so, you're a lucky devil. Always he picks Charley Company when he rides abroad. The notion of rotation — " he shrugged and let it go at that.

"Luck?" Jennings' eyebrows arched. "And ten rounds apiece!"

70

"If it comes to an engagement, you'll need to make your shots count. In such a case, try and arrange it within sight, or at least in sound, and we'll dash bravely to your rescue."

"In such a case, he won't be here to stop you," Jennings agreed, and set about his preparations. Sergeant Young's shrug was reassuring.

"It could be worse, sir. C is a better company than it was — not up to strength, and far from rejuvenated. But this new man, Corporal Abbott — he says little, but it's easy to see that he's an old hand, no tenderfoot as the Captain dubbed him at the start. There's a near-magic in the way he goes about handling the men, a knack I've never had. Already there's a new spirit in Charley Company. Given time, he would transform it."

"I guess we should be thankful for small blessings," Jennings admitted. "We're not like to have many in the days to come."

With the familiarity of long-tested friendship, Young presumed to an add comment.

"There's just a chance we've another, sir. Reports and rumors are thick as black flies in the fall, but they say this White Bear is pushing Wild Horse hard for the real leadership among the Indians. Also that the Bear is a hating man. Whereas Wild Horse, or so I've heard, is as much a gentleman as is possible for an Indian to be." In that remark he clearly found nothing incongruous. "A fair man, sir, according to his light."

71

"If it comes to the niceties between them, to keep hair on our heads, we're like to go bald early and sudden," Jennings grunted, and turned to such precautions as his orders allowed. Until now, Charley Company had been envied for the favoritism shown them, the chance to get away from the post and its monotony of duty. Today, Jennings would have cheerfully relegated so dubious a privilege to either of the other companies.

Charley Company was mustered and in formation, Sergeant Young waiting as Jennings came up. The horses seemed to stand quieter than usual, with less pawing or snorting, as though they too sensed the difference of this from former forays; or were over-tired from too many such, too many and too recent, Jennings thought grimly.

His glance rested curiously on the acting corporal, approving. Somehow there was about Abbott the easy power of a grizzly bear, batting a rotten log to pieces. Young was right. There was a difference with the Company. His suspicion that Abbott had at one time enjoyed a higher rank swung to certainty.

Captain Doorley came at a headlong gallop, swinging his horse with savage reins. Clamping its jaws, Jennings observed, on flecks of red. Cruelty was not necessarily inherent, only unthinking. Though in any case, men with red skins had no monopoly.

Doorley surveyed the company, his glance

lingering on the new corporal. His mouth tightened with displeasure at the favor which had marked the promotion, but he said nothing as he led them through the open gate. They swung south, the horses at a trot.

The eyes of sergeant and lieutenant focused on the dress sword which Doorley had buckled on, then met with grim amusement. Doorley had worn the same blade when leading his first scout, years before. Repeatedly it had gotten in his way, once all but tripping him and on subsequent occasions he had left it at home. Now it was back. Clearly he would enjoy leading a charge and waving it above his head.

Only when the horses were blowing and streaked with sweat did Doorley slacken the headlong pace. Then it was through the animals' insistence as they reached a creek that they stopped, stubbornly plunging snouts in the cool water. Jennings took it upon himself to allow the riders to dismount and drink as well.

The land lay more than usually empty as they swung south, since even the scattered settlers were at the post. Indications of desert to the west marched like warning outposts. Mist rose at midday, like dawn fog above a swamp, resolving itself into smoke as they neared. Then it was no more than a remnant, like the ashes which marked where Jose Madrone had built a house, half of logs, half of adobe. The dirt had settled, collapsing with the heat.

"Lucky for José, he's safe at the fort," Young

observed.

Abbott eyed the site appraisingly. The fire had been set at about evening of the day before.

Turning west by north, they came upon a similar reminder, followed finally by a third. At least there were no log-like objects, though at the second scene, magpies arose from clustering around a dead dog.

Doorley's face was increasingly grim. Any sense of holiday had been lost.

Observing him, Abbott felt a kindling of respect. Unfitted for command the captain certainly was, but at least he was not lacking in courage. Posturing was at least predicated on a backbone.

The sun was on a long slant to the west. At Jennings' inquiring glance, Doorley nodded grudgingly, and they halted to allow men and horses to eat. It was hardly approved procedure, but C Company had learned before that Doorley was a law unto himself.

A creek came out of the east, running soft with the lengthening summer, as though sensing that it marched to its own oblivion in thirsty sands. The thin line of brush which crowded close as though seeking reassurance furnished fuel for cooking fires, should they choose to boil coffee, to prepare a real meal. Whatever the captain had had in mind at the start, they had swung too wide and far to make it back to the fort by nightfall.

Here the land lay rumpled, the distant sheen of

occasional trees a darker, different blue from that of the sky.

"Enjoy it," Young advised Abbott. "That's the last bit of greenery, with real desert beyond. Country where the Indians can retreat at need, losing themselves beyond the finding of a white man. You'll notice the changes — the last traces of small flowers which spring only after rain, which isn't often. More prickly pear. Beyond that, the ocotillo, yucca, an occasional saguare. In a way, it's a beautiful land — as a diamond-back rattlesnake is beautiful, but unfriendly.

"This will be our closest approach. And since Indians really dislike it as much as anyone, this gathering of which there's talk will be well to the north and east — land which seems to deny that such a hell as desert could even exist. I've always wanted to see it. Maybe we will — if that's where the bear dens."

His mood was philosophical. Abbott almost regretted spoiling it, pointing out stir, a distant movement to that same north and east, but by no means far off.

"Cattle. A big herd, pushed along fast."

He did not add the obvious, that the riders would be Indians.

Jennings' startled glance was as much for him as for the distant herd. No one else had noticed.

Doorley was instant in decision and action. "Come on," he said. "We'll see about that."

Miles lay between, but the cavalry horses still had a reserve, and Doorley drove mercilessly.

That the advent of soldiers out from the south was a surprise to the raiders was soon manifest. They had not looked for trouble, at least not from that quarter nor so soon. That they were capably led was as quickly demonstrated as the big herd was expertly split, then headed in diverging directions.

It was an astute move. Charley Company was made up of good men, some of its newest recruits cattlemen themselves and furious at this latest depredation, as anxious as the captain to come to grips with the raiders. But they were still not at full strength, their horses nearing the breaking point, while those of the enemy would be fresh.

If any such thoughts occurred to Doorley he gave no indication of being bothered. He was grinning broadly, turning to fling a remark at Jennings.

"Those will be some of Wild Horse's savages. This time we'll give them a lesson! One long overdue."

Ahead, the country was increasingly broken a confusion of brush and gullies, hills and breaks. Grasslands, where summer rains turned back upon themselves, as though shuddering away from the desert. Country made for ambush, Abbott noticed, and the closing night could complete any trap into which they plunged. He could point out a herd hustled by raiders but to suggest to Doorley that a lesson might come in reverse would be frowned upon as impertinence.

Abbott was increasingly certain that Company C had been under observation most of the time since leaving the compound, their every move timed in turn. Illusions of surprise were part of a bag of tricks. Doorley had gained a false sense of confidence from being allowed on past occasions to roam unchecked.

A past as dead as they soon might be.

A darker mass spilled, rolling out of the settling night. Cattle. A startled steer whirled about to stare, then took off with tail in the air, but not before Abbott had read its brand, like an engraving on its right hip. A bar and diamond. These were Shenandoah's stock.

Chapter Nine

Though hoping for some such development, this was better luck than Wild Horse had counted on. A prudent officer, faced with such a situation, would do one of three things: the obvious, to dispatch a single scout, moving under cover of darkness, to spy and report back, while the main force remained safe behind the walls of the stockade, ready to move at need.

As a second alternative they could ride out in force, to the relief of such settlers as remained in need of help, to escort them back. But to ride wide and aimlessly, in inadequate force, was a foolishness he had hardly espected.

Yet here they were, not sensing the trap even

when sighting the bait, blundering headlong. Jennings exclaimed on a note of dismay, his voice lost in a sudden eruption of sound, the excited, triumphant yipping of warriors, the gobble of the war whoop.

Given the authority, Jennings might have managed something, but that smothered outcry was his last. His voice choked in a bubble of blood, around an arrow quivering in his throat. Doorley was cut off, enveloped by a panicky surge of cattle, swept along with them. Sergeant Young, on the flank, sensed but could not see the onset of disaster.

Abbott also sensed rather than seeing, instinct and training supplying what for the moment was indeterminate. In military annals this was as old as the clash of opposing forces, cleverly enchanced by the addition of the cattle. Having been watched from afar, the trap had been prepared, the herd of longhorns roused and moved out as they had been bedding down for the night. Here at the van they were made to serve both as shield and ram, the braves, coming behind, spilling to the attack at either side.

As strategy, it was excellent, but flawed in that the herd, rendered increasingly uneasy, were unpredictable. Abbott's advantage was a knowledge of cattle.

Shouting an order, he spurred hard, and in the absence of other leadership the suddenly apprehensive men of C Company followed. Some of the new recruits were men just in from the range, and they provided a leaven for the whole. The herd, on the verge of milling, yielded half to panic, half to push, pivoting about on themselves, their throaty bellowing drowning the sudden dismay of the warriors. It was an enveloping tactic in reverse, perfectly executed, aided by the terror of the herd, directed against itself.

No time was left for counter-ploy, for continuing attack, not even for retreat. Surprised, confused, suddenly helpless, the warriors were scattered, swept along, forced to ride for their lives. The momentum of its own rush fed the terror of the herd; from escape they swung to stampede, the drumming thunder of hoofs swelling to rocking thunder.

Jennings, dead before he spilled from the saddle, was lost, left behind along with another white man and twice that number of red. Charley Company, amid the contagion of excitement, remained disciplined as they followed Abbott and he bawled another order, keeping them to the flank of the running mass, then pulling back. The uneasy juggernaut rolled out of hearing as it already had from sight, spilling south like a widening stream.

Doorley, along with the cattle and most of the men, had been confused, blind in darkness, intent only on survival. Then, as the running horses around him slowed, he was able to think, to restore mastery of mind over body. He did not understand what had happened or how; but disaster had somehow passed them by, and in the sudden flood of light as the moon rolled above the rim of the earth, it was Abbott, not Jennings nor himself, who led.

Bewilderment mixed with amazement held Doorley speechless awhile, trying to understand the incomprehensible. His rising anger was matched by frustration, muted as a darker blot of solidity loomed off to the side. One of the newcomers, understanding what for Doorley must forever remain a mystery, pointed it out to Abbott.

"This is Miss O'Shea's ranch — those will be the buildings. They were after her cattle."

Abbott had guessed as much. Sound was again apparent, a puzzled, uncertain bawling which indicated that the frightened cattle were slowing, wondering what it was all about. In one important particular this stampede differed from those along the trail. This was home range, familiar, friendly. The dogies had turned instinctively back rather than away.

Doorley roused as from deep sleep. Anger put a bite to his voice. "Where is Mr. Jennings? Sergeant, what has happened to the Lieutenant?"

Like the others, Young had been shaken and confused, but he was among the first to recover, to understand. Exactly how a recovery had been managed he did not know, but Abbott had achieved, and whether by luck or skill made no difference. They had blundered into disaster, then been snatched back.

His reply was respectful as always.

82

"We seem to have lost him, sir. Back at the start of the mix-up, I'm afraid."

Doorley was appalled. Such a loss in itself was bad enough, but that it should be Jennings made it worse. The poor quality of the light hid the flush which suffused his face; the men had gone leaderless, without an officer. He swallowed the thought of the part he had played — or failed to.

"Did anyone see what happened? Speak up."

Abbott responded. He had a sense that it would be better to say nothing, but that much was owed to Jennings.

"Apparently he was hit by an arrow, Captain. It knocked him from his horse."

"And you left him behind, to those devils? You sounded no alarm?"

Sergeant Young interposed.

"There was no time nor opportunity, sir. In the press and confusion — "

"Did I ask your opinion, Sergeant?" Doorley shifted ground. Other matters were more immediate.

"I will inquire further into this later. Since we're here, we'll make sure that Miss O'Shea is unharmed, escort her to the protection of the fort." He angled toward the buildings. The sounds of stampede had faded.

"You'd think a light would show," Doorley grumbled. Apparently it did not occur to him that a handful of defenders might find it wiser not to call attention to their position.

Abbott studied the place as they approached.

They came in.

Abbott still looked around.

The shadowy outlines of horses crowded in a spidery corral.

Beyond the barn, outbuildings looked forlorn.

The house loomed solid and massive, built of logs, hewed and squared, a fortress in time of need.

A voice hailed from the gloom, unruffled but incisive. Abbott caught the flicker of moonlight along a rifle barrel.

"Best stop right there. Though I reckon you'll be from the fort." The voice belonged to the cowboy who had accompanied his employer to town on recent occasions.

Irritation tinged Doorley's reply. "Who else? Why should we be here except to help?"

"Mebby." The word was non-committal. "Come along in, if you like — but not more'n two or three."

Doorley was dismounting, his uncertainty forgotten. He ordered Young to come along, and the latter, after a quick glance, nodded for Abbott to join them. The events of the night had not been lost upon him.

Light made a yellow rectangle as a door was opened, then it was a different world as it closed behind them. The remnants of a supper fire smouldered in the big range, still giving out a mist of warmth. A coal oil lamp, set on a high shelf, diffused soft light. The kitchen was homey, differing from that of most ranch houses by the indefinable but unmistakable aura of a woman's touch.

Shenandoah, without a sunbonnet, showed proud head crowned by vivid flame of hair, softly piled. The green eyes were watchful as a cat's, yet with the same almost sleepy composure. As though unconscious of the disturbance so lately transpiring without, or careless of it, she sat back comfortably in a heavy wooden rocker. She had been occupied, not with a rifle, but with needle and thread, mending some garment as dainty yet as serviceable as herself.

Doorley was taken aback. Clearly he had looked for apprehension if not outright panic. An angular woman appeared to survey the newcomers from a side door, her hair equally neat but gray. She made no attempt to hide her unease, matched by determination. She held a shotgun.

Shenandoah did not rise. Her glance ranged to Young, lingered a moment on Abbott, then returned to Doorley as the latter glared at Abbott, surprise and outrage in his eyes. Her voice was even, without emotion. "To what do we owe the honor of this visit, Captain?"

Doorley spluttered. To his mind, everyone was behaving insanely. "No honor, Miss Shenandoah. Necessity. For one thing, your cattle were being driven away by the Indians. We chased them off and brought back the herd."

Clearly his claim came as no surprise. A sharp watch was kept here. Shenandoah was matter-of-fact.

"In that case, I am grateful. I fear we were taken rather by surprise."

She was not the only one, Young thought admiringly. It had been an evening of surprises.

Doorley was exasperated. "Surely you can understand your danger? I'm gratified that matters have been no worse, but you and the others here must return with us to the post, immediately. It is the only possible course."

Shenandoah laid aside her sewing and arose. Her bearing was unconsciously regal. "I'm grateful for your concern, Captain, but as I have told you before, I have no intention of deserting my home or neglecting my ranch. We are prepared to defend ourselves if the necessity should arise."

Mrs. Pedersen, who clearly served both as housekeeper and companion, had laid aside the shotgun. Bustling about the range, she wielded a coffee-pot, and the aroma filled the room as she poured several cups-full.

"You gentlemen will be thirsty," she suggested.

Though annoyed at the interruption, Doorley retained the instincts of a gentleman. He bowed acknowledgement, accepting a cup, seating himself. The others followed suit. But he refused to condescend to small talk at such a time, sipping the coffee sternly.

"I must remind you, both of you, that there is no time to waste. We will wait long enough for you to secure a small pack of personal belongings, but that is all."

"Don't let us delay you." Shenandoah was remote. "Since we are not going."

Doorley all but choked, still incredulous. "Not going? But can't you understand? It is imperative, necessary — "

Shenandoah was every inch a lady, but she was also a woman accustomed to command, running a big outfit and apparently doing it well. Her hair should have made clear to Doorley that she did not suffer fools, gladly or otherwise.

"It is you who do not seem to understand, Captain. This is my house, my ranch. I intend to remain."

"But that's impossible. I can't permit it. You must come along — "

The green eyes blazed with sudden fury.

"Must? You forget yourself, sir. Or do you have in mind to use force, as you so high-handedly have compelled everyone else to your whims, when they entrusted themselves to the protection of the fort?"

Doorley's cheeks reddened, then went white. Unchecked power had gone to his head.

"I don't like the words you use, Madam, but for your own protection, I intend to assure your safety — "

Abbott had less trouble in understanding. Even while not admitting it to himself, Doorley had the uncomfortable awareness of having played a poor part in the night's events. If for no other reason than his self-respect, he could not back down.

Shenandoah understood, though not so clearly. She was outraged by such boorishness, his assumption of authority bounded only by his own decision. She swung to Young and Abbott.

"Sergeant, Corporal, are you mean, or merely puppets because of your position? This is my land, my house, and some of you are interlopers. Surely, as officers and gentlemen, you have a higher duty than to back a madman in such folly?"

Her choice of words cut like whips. Doorley was staggered. Young moved uncertainly, and Doorley vented his wrath on him.

"Sergeant! Don't forget your position. I'll permit no insubordination with the necessary execution of my orders! As for you," he added bitterly to Abbott, "you seemed about to say something?"

"There's a deal I might say," Abbott shrugged. He had restrained himself for the common good, but there was a limit. "But Miss O'Shea has said it already, and better. Your actions have been high-handed, and how a board of inquiry, or even a court-martial, might view them, is questionable. I'm willing to serve as a part of the army for the duration of this emergency, but you are overstepping both your authority and good judgement. I stand with the lady, that she has rights which you have no authority to transgress, certainly not by force."

Doorley was taken aback. That was plain

speaking. Infuriated but to some degree intimidated, he covered his retreat with bluster. "I certainly would not constrain a woman by force, even for her own good. As for you, you're wearing the insignia of a corporal, and as such you have grossly overstepped all privilege. Sergeant, that man is under arrest."

With a jerk of the head to Shenandoah, he stalked from the house.

Chapter Ten

Blackjack McQuade gnawed at his fingernails, a bad habit of which he had long since broken himself, save that it recurred in moments of extreme stress. Tonight was the night for delivering the contraband rifles to the Indians, completing the transaction begun months before. The date had been loosely agreed upon, conveniently subject to change, until forced upon him by Wild Horse's insistance. If he failed to make good, the chief wuld be more than wild. Any unbroken bronco would be mild by comparison.

Captain Doorley's error of judgement was commonly blamed for the increasing trouble, but

McQuade knew that it had merely speeded a movement already under way. Wild Horse, knowing white men better than most of his people, trusted them less. Unwillingly he had come to the conclusion that it was a case of fight or die. That the odds were heavy he shrugged aside; death in battle was honorable and could be easier. It was a case of drive out the invaders, or be overrun.

The timing of the uprising had initially depended on when McQuade could supply the rifles. Other factors, other men, notably the Bear, had intervened, but even if Wild Horse had seen no reason to change, events had gotten out of hand. With repeating rifles and ammunition, he would have a double advantage, not only of surprise but of superior fire-power. Without the latter, their cause would be lost before it was begun.

At this stage he would brook no delay.

Since to furnish such rifles was a risky, almost a treasonable business, running them in not only under the eyes of the soldiers but with the protection of the army, McQuade had required a powerful persuader — a premium price, paid in gold, half in advance.

He had not inquired as to where or how Wild Horse would get the money. The chief had managed.

Now it was up to McQuade to make good on his end of the deal. He had resisted the chief's urging to smuggle out a few rifles at a time as being too dangerous. The knowledge of them would spread, a warning to the army which would lead to a search, inevitably narrowing to his store.

He had promised delivery of the entire consignment at the proper time. Wild Horse had concurred.

This was the night. The warriors would be coming, and unless the rifles were ready, Wild Horse would be unable to constrain his men — nor would he wish to. And the target of their wrath would be McQuade.

McQuade's plan had been simple, easy — until events had gotten out of hand. Doorley's orders, in consequence, had been strict. The gates were to remain shut.

The sentry to whom McQuade had supplied whiskey and cigars was not on duty tonight. His replacement was as dour as the name he bore, Jock McIvor. He listened respectfully to McQuade's request, but his head-shake was obdurate. "Good reasons you may have, Mr. McQuade, sorr. I'll na dispute the point. But it canna be done. Orders is orders. The gate on no occasion is to be opened — certainly not for the passage outward of men or wagons!"

"But this is business," McQuade protested. "I'm the sutler, and my contract requires me to provide necessary supplies for the post. When that wagon broke down, some of the supplies had to be unloaded, left behind. I've just learned that there were guns among them — repeating rifles.

I've just finished checking the shortage, and made sure. You can see what that would mean, if some of the red devils came upon them before we can recover them!"

It was a potent argument. For the warring Comanche to have better guns than the soldiers —

A lesser or less stubborn man might have been persuaded. McIvor did not even waver.

"It's sorry I am, sorr. But orders ir orders. Unless one of the lieutenants, or even the major, brings me different, then those of the captain must stand."

McQuade choked on an oath. As well reach for the moon, now sailing majestically overhead. He turned at the clop of hoofs and grate of wheels, as the laden wagon loomed out of the dusk, then halted. He had counted on his powers of persuasion and his assistant, Corrigan, could be counted on. He loomed on the seat like a colossus, possessing ears to rival a fox's. Always a man for action, requiring no orders in such an emergency, he kicked on the brake, wrapping the reins about its handle, then jumped with surprising lightness to the ground. Jock McIvor, addressing McQuade, failed to see what Corrigan clutched in ham-size fist.

He collapsed without a sound as Corrigan struck with the hammer side of a hatchet.

"Shall I load him aboard?" Corrigan asked.

McQuade understood. The boy could not be left to tell its story. Corrigan would turn the unconscious man over to the Indians as a sort of bonus.

McQuade was not revolted. But there was a better way.

"Get the gate open and move the wagon," he instructed, and took the hatchet from Corrigan's fingers. It was one of a score of dozen, included with the rifles. The Indians were paying a premium price, having discovered the efficiency of such tools as scalping hatchets.

McQuade dragged the unconscious sentry to the far side of the gate. The hatchet was indeed a handy tool. The horses shied at the sudden scent of fresh blood as Corrigan drove them through, then closed the gate. The post slept, undisturbed.

McQuade straightened, the dripping scalp in his hand. When the body should be found that would be a convincing touch. And the trophy should please Wild Horse.

A white man would have vented his fury in wild gesture or bitter complaint. The chief did neither. Jaw hard-set, his face inscrutable, he leaned low along the neck of his pony, the cayuse increasing its speed like a jack-rabbit. The warriors still followed, equally disgruntled at the turn of events, but unquestioning. To them it appeared that Wild Horse, cheated of the herd, intended to attack the fort. Surprise might compensate for the foolhardiness of such an attempt.

Wild Horse had no such notion. One failure was enough for a night. Exactly how that had come about he would never fully understand, knowing little of cattle or the unreasoning impulses by which they moved, not aware how Abbott had turned those to account.

The chief's initial impulse had been to regather his own men, to pursue the soldiers and attack. Reason had prevailed. Even though it had lost its officer, someone was leading C Company effectively, and so brash an encounter might prove disastrous. In any event, it would delay them to the point where the far more vital delivery of the rifles might be jeopardized.

Wild Horse placed no trust in Blackjack McQuade, only in the certainty that it was as much to the sutler's interests as his own to complete the delivery and collect his pay. That he dealt with a villain had been patent from the outset. His only surprise had been that those in charge at the fort should remain so blind and easily hoodwinked; but the almost fatal illness of the Major, the headlong blundering of the Captain, had played into McQuade's hands and his own.

McQuade would bring out the guns, not alone for the money still to be paid, but because he had gone too far to turn back. The scales, for a while delicately balanced, had tipped.

McQuade had reached the same conclusion. Up to a few hours before, he had intended to make full use of his position, an influence rivaling that of the man in command, to send out the wagon with Corrigan at the reins, and so satisfy his obligations with a minimum risk that his part might ever become known. His apprehension had mounted at the increasing number of rifles in his store, which mischance might reveal. With them gone, so was the risk. No one could connect him with the uprising of a bunch of wild-crazy warriors.

He had been prepared thereafter, when others failed — especially and particularly Captain Doorley — to lead a rescue and save Shenandoah, covering himself with glory and earning her gratitude. From that point forward, his fortune made, he would follow the paths of rectitude.

Now those well-laid plans had come to ruin. Partly it had been the headlong blundering of Doorley, with his assumption of authority, partly to that blasted newcomer, Abbott. Somehow he had exerted a quiet influence, which at times had been decisive.

All at once it was impossible to go back, and the worst of that was that long-dreamed plan which had included Shenandoah. But there were more roads than one to a destination.

In other aspects he had provided against such a contingency. The wagon contained not alone three hundred repeating rifles and boxes of cartridges, even hatchet — but tucked away in a corner of the high box was a heavy sack, spendable proceeds of the deal to date.

His only real regret was that Shenandoah must come to know him for what he was. But to forever play at being a gentleman was perhaps beyond him. This other was more to his liking.

The early moon had climbed as though eager for a better point from which to view what was transpiring. The stockade walls were dim with distance. Out of the west a shadow moved along the ground, even with no cloud to cast it. Horsemen. That would be Wild Horse and his men, according to appointment.

Something — chance, hunch or premonition — caused McQuade to look farther to the side, to stiffen between dismay and comprehension. Off there was a second group, and both were riding hard, the wagon a common target.

There could hardly be rival groups of Indians, so the explanation was forced upon him. Unlike Wild Horse, who had remained silent in the face of surprise, McQuade swore.

The last thing that he had expected or calculated was that Captain Doorley might discover either the wagon or the warriors, or head to intercept the wagon, to a clash with the Comanches. He had ruled Doorley out as too inept, too far away in any case.

Now his plans, already in disarray, were threatened with ruin.

"Wait," he ordered Corrigan, and jumped down, then ran to where he had provided against such possible mischance, to a saddled horse tied at the rear of the wagon. Grunting with the effort, he retrieved and hoisted the sack of money, tying it behind the saddle.

"You don't know a thing about anything," he

flung at Corrigan, who for the first time showed signs of nervousness. "All you do is drive for me. That lets you out."

Before Corrigan could frame a protest, McQuade was riding for such shadows as were available. Now he'd lose that final payment for the rifles, but to be caught by the men of Charley Company, with those guns in the wagon, and the Indians riding to beat them to the rifles —

Should he live that long, it would be to face a firing squad at dawn.

Chapter Eleven

Abbott, as usual, had been the one to sight the wagon, perhaps because he was looking for it; still remembered years of war had been made up of watches in the silent hours, of forays by night and to eyes initially keener than those of most others had been added experience, a judgment of what shadows might mean.

He pointed out the wagon to Sergeant Young, who wasted no time with pointless speculation. It might, of course, belong to some settler, tardy in seeking the shelter of the fort. But against so reasonable a likelihood was the evidence that the wagon was not heading for, but away from such a haven.

Young managed to convey that pertinent fact respectfully, in a swift report to Captain Doorley.

"A wagon off there, sir — and swinging to AVOID the fort, from the look of it."

Doorley was instantly concerned. Such conduct at such a time was highly suspicious.

"Then we'd better have a look at it," he decided, and swung to lead.

Abbott's second discovery, moments later, of another mass of horsemen, also heading for the wagon, required no pointing out. They were too many and moving too fast to escape observation. Doorley was bewildered.

"What do you make of them, Sergeant?"

"Indians, sir. Whether they're the same bunch we tangled with before, or not, they've just about got to be Comanches."

Such logic was indisputable. And their interest in the wagon was clear, though its intensity was harder to understand.

"Some fool of a settler," Doorley grumbled. "But we can't allow them to take his scalp."

That a headlong clash must result, probably with considerable loss of life on each side, did not deter him. He was a soldier. Still, it paid to be prudent.

"If they're foolish enough to make a fight of it, we'll hit 'em hard. But flankingly," he added That could be most devastating, yet avoid the carnage of a direct clash.

Abbott understood his thinking, and in general approved the tactic. The trouble was that the wagon might well be cut out in such a maneuver.

"Begging the Captain's pardon, sir, but I doubt if that is a settler's outfit. It looks to be a supply wagon from the fort."

Doorley's eyebrows contracted instinctively, for the remark held the seeds of suggestion if not advice. Then he was forced to the same conclusion, and that altered the situation. How or why such a wagon should be out here, heading away from the fort, he could not understand, but it had the smell of mutiny. He bristled.

"We'll drive straight for the wagon," he amended. It was easy to ignore Abbott.

Wild Horse was equally startled. The last thing that he had expected was that the soldiers would cross their path a second time that night, or guess at the importance of the wagon. But it was happening, and in this were elements of disaster.

Not only were his warriors outnumbered, but the cavalrymen would be in an ugly mood. Under such conditions a headlong battle might be disastrous; it would at least ruin all chance at the rifles, which were his primary objective.

They had to come first. If the rifles were lost so might the war be, at its inception. Battles are not often fought according to the well laid plans of generals or staff. Chance rides a black horse.

There was no trace of cloud across the star-studded expanse of sky, nothing to hide the moon. So far as light was concerned, they would fight on even terms.

Jack rabbits had sprung to frenzied leaping at the sudden onrush of horses. Several bounded away, ghostly as the puff of cannon smoke above a battlefield. A night bird, beating on frantic wings, screamed its displeasure. The drum-beat of hoofs stirred bitter dust, coating faces, eyes and nostrils, rendering mouths grotesque.

Both groups of horses had run long and far, and their riders were equally tired. Chance favored the cavalry, in that they had a lesser distance to cover. Wild Horse recognized the disadvantage but kept driving. Most of his warriors were armed only with bows and arrows, a few with rifles. Those were smooth-bores or muzzle loaders, a motley collection.

But it was the owner of such a weapon who thought first to use it, sending the bullet screaming just over the heads of the men in blue. Abbott and Young alike had wondered at Doorley's restraint in withholding fire so long. That he had forgotten to give the order shamed him to a quick flush, unnoticed in the half-dark. He barked an order, now, and despite the difficulty of aiming from running horses at targets racing with equal speed, the point-blank range counted. Three Indian ponies ran riderless.

It was devastating to braves largely untried, ill-equipped to match such fire-power. They broke and scattered, only a few returning the shots.

Doorley was gripped by the excitement of conflict. Even in that moment of triumph, it came to him that he was building a reputation for Charley Company and for himself.

On the wagon, Corrigan watched with a lively interest which altered to dismay. The sudden desertion of McQuade had warned him, though he did not particularly blame his employer. As a hired hand, he might explain, even be excused, which McQuade could not. Though whether anyone would believe was another matter.

The realization that the soldiers were winning the skirmish was in no way reassuring. Those guns would be difficult to explain, and that on such a night foray he could have been ignorant of them or their purpose would be too wild an excuse even to propound.

The heavily loaded wagon could neither run nor fight. But he could do one, if denied the other. That suited Corrigan. He was not a man to run.

The light was good, as the others swept closer. Understanding came to Corrigan. Abbott was in the forefront, heading straight for the wagon, even as Captain Doorley swung away, leading the bulk of his followers in pursuit of the Indians.

Corrigan reached for a rifle, lying at the bottom of the wagon box. Abbott was coming up too fast. Corrigan changed his mind, snatching instead for the hatchet which he and McQuade had used jointly against Jock McIvor. The bright sheen of its blade showed dimmed and stained.

Abbott's horse stumbled, so that his shot missed. Corrigan heard its sound of passage as he cocked his arm.

McQuade had watched from a short distance, not daring to keep his horse to a run, thereby calling attention to himself. His face contorted at sight of Abbott, understanding even as did his employee. In the confusion of battle he could do a necessary chore and no one the wiser. He lifted his revolver and squeezed on the trigger.

The sudden move of the team jerked the wagon to motion, the violence spoiling Corrigan's aim. The hatchet spun past Abbott's eyes. And McQuade's bullet, well aimed, made a red spatter of Corrigan's face as the moving wagon drew him between.

Chapter Twelve

Doorley witnessed it, between incredulity and dismay. McQuade was gone, taking advantage of the night and confusion, and it was clear enough that he had been involved, though why or how, Doorley did not understand. He stared in sour disbelief. "You're lucky to be alive, soldier. That shot was intended for you. Though what it's all about, what McQuade was doing out here in the first place — "

He broke off, striving to retrieve some remnant of dignity. The raiders had been driven off, not once but twice, still the night was almost a disaster.

"Take a look at what's inside the wagon,"

Abbott invited, and lifted the canvas flap at the rear. "It pretty well explains the whole business, sir — why the Indians were so anxious to reach it, and what McQuade was doing."

Suspiciously, Doorley complied, slow to accept even the evidence of his own eyes. That gun-running on such a scale could have been carried on while he was in charge at the fort seemed incredible; also it reflected upon him. But added reflection eased the sting. The final and decisive deal had been thwarted, by the force which he led. Much of the credit would be his.

Even better, McQuade was exposed for the scoundrel which Doorley had always accounted him, no longer a rival or a counter to his influence. Doorley was almost jovial.

"That was good work on your part," he admitted. Matters had worked out so well that he could afford to be magnanimous. "You've gone part way toward redeeming yourself. I'll take such factors into consideration."

He had not revoked the order of arrest, Abbott reflected, as they swung toward the fort. For the moment he was too tired to care. Smoke was lifting when they turned in at the gate, the cooks getting breakfast on the fire. The outlines of the settlers wagons were taking shape. The fretful voice of an uneasy child seemed strangely out of place.

Appraised of the company's return, DeKalb, sleepy-eyed and unshaven, was at hand to greet them. Doorley took the salute, drawing himself up with an effort. A day and a night in the saddle took toll.

"Sergeant, you will take charge of the wagon, with particular attention to its contents," he instructed Young, then remembered to turn back to DeKalb with what had become a perfunctory inquiry regarding the commandant. The reply startled him.

"I am happy to be able to inform you that Major Connoly shows greatly improved, sir. He has left standing orders for you to report to him, immediately upon your return."

"Immediately? But at this hour?" Doorley was incredulous. "Your news is most encouraging, but he will need his sleep — "

"Everyone was aroused by the noise of battle, sir. He is awake."

Doorley obeyed the summons, responding with a sense of unease. He was pleased, of course, more than happy, at so encouraging a report. But the realization that he would no longer be in command came as a shock. He had come to think of himself as in charge.

An additional night and day, with a reasonably hearty meal as the old day had waned, had restored Connoly to a surprising degree. He was propped up in bed, waiting between eagerness and impatience for Doorley's report. Doorley stared, then commenced an effusive torrent of surprise and congratulation. Connoly cut him short with a gesture of exasperation.

"Of course, and thank you, but never mind

about that now, Captain. Your report, if you please."

"Er — of course, sir. Though I'm afraid it will be rather a long story, to cover all that has occurred — ."

"In that case, it can wait. I don't see Mr. Abbott. I thought he would be with you."

"Abbott? With me?" Doorley was taken aback. Connoly's reference was the last thing he would have expected.

"We do have a temporary recruit of that name," he added uncertainly. "I may say that he is under arrest, for a variety of infractions, including insubordination — "

The door opened, and Lieutenant Van Dyke entered hurriedly, accompanied by Abbott. He saluted.

"Here he is, Major, according to your orders. Mr. Abbott. He has just now returned, along with — "

Major Connoly was still too weak to spring from his bed, but it was apparent to the onlookers that he would have done so had that been possible. Face glowing, he held out both hands in a gesture of welcome.

"Montana! Bill Montana, you're a sight for sore eyes!"

Abbott was across the room, to grip those outstretched hands, his voice suddenly hoarse. His seldom-seen smile matched the Major's.

"John! It's good to find you better."

Hands gripping, they eyed each other

110

delightedly, then, as the excitement was replaced by tiredness, Abbott stepped back and the Major sank to the pillows, grumbling.

"Better, if you call being weak as an infernal kitten anything to shout about. But the news that you were here has been a tonic. I sent for you yesterday, but you were gone." He wasted no more words with welcome or question.

"Gentlemen, allow me to introduce Captain Montana Abbott, my long-time friend and fellow-officer. From what little I have been able to find out or understand, Bill, a bad situation hereabouts has grown worse during my incapacity. For the present I'm too confoundedly weak to go into matters but from now I'll have the satisfaction of knowing that they are in competent hands.

"Since it appears that you are back in the service, however irregularly, we will go on from there. As Senior Captain, you will assume full charge here at the post, taking whatever action you deem necessary or expedient. Gentlemen, I trust that is clear?"

A touch of color had returned to his washed-out cheeks, but his eyes closed wearily. Montana was deeply moved, as surprised by so sweeping a declaration as any. He clasped a hand in mute reassurance, then nodded to the others and led the way out.

Doorley moved as in a trance. The revelations in what little Connoly had said were as shocking as they had been unexpected. It came to him that he had been over-zealous, perhaps indiscreet. Connoly had not reprimanded him but clearly he was displeased with what he had learned.

Now, he was abruptly under the command and at the mercy of a man upon whom he had visited a petty sense of jealousy, going out of his way to humiliate him. Just as clearly, should Abbott choose to reverse the situation, Doorley could look for no sympathy from Connoly.

Montana Abbott! He had heard the name somewhere but had never connected it with the Abbott who had drifted in, a man he'd assumed to be a tenderfoot. That had been another mistake.

Then, for the second time that morning, Doorley squared tired shoulders, swinging about, saluting as smartly as he could manage.

"It appears that I have made a fool of myself, sir. What are your orders?"

Abbott returned the steady look from fatigue-reddened eyes. On the frayed rim of exhaustion, as was the case with Doorley, he felt a spark of respect, almost of liking, for this headlong but well-meaning man. Somewhere his training had been deficient, but character had a way of cropping up when it came to the crunch. Doorley had the makings of a good officer.

"I intend to get some sleep, Captain," Montana returned. "My suggestion would be for you to do the same."

He had not come by the name Blackjack by

chance. McQuade, fumbling cartridges from his belt and stuffing them into the chambers of his revolver as he rode, was in full control of his emotions as he surveyed the coming dawn. Blackjack was a gambler's game, requiring a cool head and the taking of chances. Even so, and with the realization that the luck of a night could become the doom of a day, he was conscious of a premonitory, uncomfortable prickling sensation at the roots of his scalp.

That his bullet, intended for Abbott, had strayed somehow to kill Corrigan, was too bad; not so much for the mischance to the driver, but that Abbott had escaped. That pestilential fellow had a surprising run of luck —

And why not? Abbott! Of course! Montana Abbott!

That explained a lot, though not all. But the fellow's luck was almost proverbial.

The devil of it was that a man had a lot to do with making his luck, good or bad. If only he hadn't missed —

To have been able to point out to Wild Horse that Abbott was dead, and by his hand, would have gone far to redress, almost to balance the situation. But to attempt to explain or excuse such a failure would be a waste of breath, exciting contempt.

The men of Charley Company, along with the wagon and the rifles, were heading back for the fort. The chief and his disgruntled warriors had scattered, but not to the point where his own escape would be easy or even possible. In the growing light they had already seen him; some few swinging to intercept him, and that would be at Wild Horse's order. McQuade held his pony to a walk. His appearance of profound thought was only partly a pose.

Comanche honor had been dragged in the dust. That they had failed twice in a night through sheer mischance shed no more glory upon McQuade than upon them; Wild Horse would know that, but any explanation or excuse would be a show of weakness. The mood of the braves was as savage and unpredictable as themselves.

Still they showed restraint as they closed around the sutler, looking to their leader to unleash them. The thoughts of Wild Horse must match his name.

His greeting as McQuade came up was like the first low note of warning growl in the throat of a wolf.

"Rifles! As empty as promises!"

McQuade shrugged. To make the gesture natural required all the resolution he could summon. But Indians respected courage. Also, like a wolf-pack at a show of fear, they would spring to attack.

"The rifles were in the wagon. Am I to blame that you came late?"

Wild Horse recognized the justice in that. The fault had not been McQuade's.

"My men — like myself — are in evil mood, seeing only the dark side. We are in a temper for

114

war, yet we lack the the weapons with which to fight."

McQuade breathed easier. He had feared the initial reaction, a swift arrow or stroke of war axe. "I'm of a mind to match. Because of what I did, and with the guns still in the wagon, the hand of every pale face will be against me. I can not return."

Wild Horse grunted. Immersed in his own woes, that aspect had not occurred to him. But he did not proffer sanctuary among his own people.

"We have a war," he pointed out somberly. "There can now be no drawing back, even were we so minded. But to fight, it will be difficult."

McQuade's mind was outrunning him. He had no choice but to work with the Indians, no longer half-heartedly or from a sheltered position. What had seemed at the outset to be a safe gamble, a sure thing, had backfired. His survival was at stake, so to assure it he must make himself invaluable.

There was a way. He shrank from the thought, but this was life or death. Whatever the cost to others.

"The feet of those who wear the moccasins are swift," he observed, reverting to the vernacular of the red man. "Like the return of wild geese after winter, reports have reached my ears, strange tales of another red man — a warrior-prophet, who has come out of the east. Tales full of wonder."

Wild Horse nodded, his eyes suddenly as hooded as those of a hawk.

"The tales you will have heard are of the White Bear — the great one who has been expected, he who some call Son of the Sun." His voice was a mixture of restraint, hope, even fear. "Such reports drift like dust stirred by the wind, and for a long while I closed my ears to them, as to rumors only. But unbelief lightened to doubt. Now I wonder — but almost I believe."

"Then it is true, a spiritual leader comes out from the East? And of course he will have heard of you, of your valor and exploits, of your will to fight. No doubt he sends you proffer of alliance?"

He was probing, purely at a venture, to distract attention from the loss of the rifles. Surprisingly, Wild Horse nodded.

"I have received messages from him, a call to listen when the voices speak and if I find them true, to join with him. Because I scoffed, I have been humbled for my disbelief." He was surprisingly contrite. "The bold stroke which I envisioned has fallen short."

"I listen," McQuade said simply.

Wild Horse was in a mood to unburden himself. And as on other occasions, he was impressed by the scope of the sutler's knowledge, the cold-blooded capacity of the man.

"It has been a dream, among the great leaders of my people, almost from the time when white men first set foot upon the sunrise shores, to

116

unite as one nation against them, to sweep them again into the sea. Many have tried. Chiefs such as King Philip; Pontiac; Tecumseh; Opechancanough; Black Hawk. The list is long. A record both of gallantry — and for this reason I hesitate — of failure.

"But the tradition among our peoples is that one day the true leader will come, one who will succeed. And it must be soon, else it will be too late! So now there is this White Bear — a strange name, since he is of the Cat People. They are a branch of the Eries, of the Six Nations. But these Eries at one time dominated the Long House, their priesthood unlike that of all others, with magic unknown to most. For more than a century they caused the frontiers to run with blood. Now this White Bear makes the claim to being a priest of the old tradition, sent by the Great Spirit to redeem his people. I doubted — and am punished for my lack of faith."

"So he invites you to meet with him, to listen to the prophecies, to combine forces?"

"All that, and more. The report is that warriors of many tribes and nations, inspired by my example and believing his promises, are flocking to join him. I begin to see that the time for war was not yet. It was distracting me and my people from that journey."

Rationalizing his set-back, he had determined on the other. McQuade was more than pleased. "I too, am one of you," he reminded. "Else why would I risk all as I have done, to help? Let us

117

make the journey together. And we will have something of value to take to that meeting. A hostage of value where the soldiers are concerned. Even without that," his voice rose on a note of anger. "Who has been most responsible for what went wrong with your plans and mine? Who but this red-headed woman who scorns white men and red alike?"

The chief's involuntary grip on his horse's rein checked the animal. His eyes gleamed with understanding, a questing eagerness like a hound's. He was suddenly eager, ranging ahead.

"The woman called Shenandoah, she whose eyes are cat's eyes, whose hair is the crimson of blood still to be shed! It is a good idea. Better," he added, and surveyed McQuade with deliberate malice, "than you know."

McQuade felt a qualm of doubt. He had counted on the chief realizing the value of Shenandoah as a hostage, which would place her beyond the reach of Doorley and Abbott, and leave him in the role of protector. He had not worked out the scheme beyond those initial stages but if it was not entirely to his liking, at least it offered possibilities which he was confident of being able to exploit.

Now he wondered if he had miscalculated. Something which he had not counted on seemed to please Wild Horse inordinately.

"I do not understand," he confessed.

"Already the peoples are responding to the summons of the Prophet, journeying toward a meeting-place at the new Western Long House, there to listen to the Bear, to listen to the prophecies, to behold the working of his magic. For only by great medicine, strong magic, along with many fighting men, can the venture upon which we are embarking be made to succeed."

The sounded reasonable, but McQuade had little interest in such details.

"But what has the girl to do with that?"

"Everything." The scope of his answer was staggering. "The White Bear is a priest of the ancient order, of the Cat People who dwelt by the lakes. Even now he makes strong medicine. But even he must have a woman to dream for him — and to interpret his own dreams! A priestess, according to the rites of the ancient tradition."

Despite the rising heat of the sun, McQuade felt cold. "I still do not see."

"Is my white brother so obtuse?" Wild Horse mocked. "I am sure that you begin to understand. No ordinary woman can serve as priestess at such a time. Only one very special, set apart for that destiny, marked as the possessor of hidden powers. The Bear has searched zealously to discover the one! And the tongue of a white man speaks the hitherto hidden truth!"

"But I didn't mean — what truth, what sign?"

"A white-skinned woman, pale as the stars at night, with skin white as milk! Hair which flames like fire, the token of the blood to be shed, her eyes the green of the Cat, the night-creatures!

"You have spoken, perhaps unwittingly, but that is the way of those who prophesy. It is made clear. We shall journey to the Long House, taking her with us, delivering her to the Bear to serve as his priestess, to prophesy."

Men and horses were tired, but Wild Horse swung purposefully.

Chapter Thirteen

Abbott slept for a couple of hours, then awakened as if on signal. He had not consciously willed to rouse at that hour, but a warning sense sounded alarm. Without hesitation he knew what it was, with the fear that already it might be too late.

"Wild Horse, or maybe McQuade, will think of her sooner or later, red hair, green eyes and all — a fine gift at the very least for the White Bear, and what more — "

He stifled a groan. No wonder his sleep had been cut short, even without dreams. And that could be the key. A woman who dreamd; every Indian whom he had known placed great store on dreams and their interpretation, as a vital link between the real and the spirit world, which to them were almost interchangeable, coupled with the powers of the spirit. By whatever name it was called, medicine or hope, by such processes lives and destinies were shaped.

Montana had come in part to understand and in considerable measure to accept. That the red man's approach to the unseen should differ from the white man's was natural, but a common instinct was in the heart of every man.

John Connoly had napped, and was refreshed. He listened without surprise as Abbott explained, including his apprehensions.

"I wasn't thinking straight, though that is no excuse. If I've blundered, I'll have to do the best I can to rectify it, and hope it's not past repair. You can see how much worse this may make an already bad situation. It's not merely her own life, though that's more than enough, but it could be the real match to powder."

Connoly nodded. "I hadn't thought of that, but you could be right. I'll not delay you an added moment, when each minute may count so much. But if you are too late already — "

"Then they'll head for the Long House — and so will I."

The Major forebore to point out the perils inherent in such a course. Montana would understand no man better. He turned instead to the practical. "How? No one — no white man, at least — knows its location. And not many

122

Indians. If any of my guides could show you, I'd send them, and gladly. They'd do no better than myself. Even you, without a guide, could wander like the Children of Israel in the wilderness and just as lost."

Montana nodded grim acceptance.

"And waste time, with none to spare. I'll tell you something, John, since in any case the secret no longer matters. The man in charge of Indian affairs is not the fool which some account him. He has seen hearing the same tales as you and I and what he hears worries him. Somewhere out from here — and to that extent his information was positive — is a man, perhaps the one Indian who knows where the Long House is, aside from the followers of the Bear. The one man who might lead me there, because of ancient enmity between the Cat People and his own: a Mohican."

To his surprise, Connoly nodded, then supplied the name. "Running Wolf."

"You know him?"

"I have heard of him."

"I was persuaded to head out here, to find him — and persuade him in turn. Now, it is more vital than ever."

Major Connoly extended a thin white hand, but its clasp was still vital. He had no need for more questions or explanation. If both Montana and the man in charge of Indian affairs considered this so important, their convictions only matched his own.

"Luck to you, Bill." He became official. "You have full authority to do whatever you think best, to act as necessary to control the situation before it gets completely out of hand."

Montana returned the grip. "I'm riding for the ranch."

He picked three men to go along, from the settlers who had congregated at the fort. Charley Company, along with Captain Doorley, were getting a much-needed rest.

He rode with a loose rein, resisting the impulse to spur. A good pony deserved consideration. In any case, it could cover a span of miles in less time at a steady pace than by a wild burst leading to exhaustion.

Nothing stirred. The ranch buildings stood intact, but that brought no reassurance. The time of day was reason enough for no smoke from chimneys. But the silence continued as Abbott dismounted and rapped sharply at the door, then shoved impatiently when there was no response.

A chair lay overturned, the only evidence of struggle. The house was empty.

There were no horses in barn or corrals. Then a man pointed to where horsemen came at an easy jog, returning members of the crew. Busy with rounding up the strayed herd, they had been out all night.

One of the total was missing, and he had remained at the buildings. They found the body among a clump of weeds beyond a shed. Flies covered the bloody gash where the scalp had been ripped away.

Montana had seen the morning-after carnage of battle on other occasions, but never had he felt sicker, or looked to the future with greater apprehension. The virtual certainty that, even had he headed directly for the ranch rather than the fort, he would probably have arrived tardily, was no comfort. Or even that he had made that trip to the post guarded and under arrest.

But they had taken Mrs. Pedersen as well, as friend and companion to Shenandoah, and that, coupled with the cirumstances, placed them above the ordinary run of captives. The trouble was that such a basis for hope was added reason for fear.

Putting together a small pack from the supplies of storeroom and kitchen, he issued his orders. "They've left the buildings intact, instead of burning them," he pointed out. "Not because they expect to allow her to return, but because to them she is something special. I doubt if they'll bother here or in this vicinity again, at least not soon. So you fellows keep on looking after the ranch.

"The rest of you, report back to Major Connoly."

Alone, he could travel faster, with less chance of discovery. Initially, his greatest handicap was his unfamiliarity with the country. But none of these others knew much more than himself.

On the previous foray, ranging with Charley Company, there had been a sense of unseen eyes, of a not quite tangible presence. Today that was gone. The land lay empty, deserted. Wild Horse and his warriors had made no effort to conceal the signs of their departure, but the ground, hard-baked from weeks of summer sun, was stingy with clues. Moreover they had ridden widely dispersed, as though to spread the word, to gather in others from west and east.

A gathering like clouds, to mass and darken, breaking like storm across the land. Wild Horse, goaded to fury, had acted prematurely, but their strike would become a spearhead for rebellion, under the Bear — prophet and priest, Son of the Sun. A local unrest could blaze to far-spread war under one who was the possessor through inheritance and tradition of the secrets of an ancient priesthood, a medicine man.

In other words, Abbott reflected his magic would be successful according to the savagery with which it was rendered.

White Bear boasted descent from the Eries, a tribe of the Six Nations, builders of houses, tillers of the soil; of the Long House, deep hidden in a remote wilderness, whence warfare had been directed over a century against white men across a thousand trackless miles.

In the days of the Revolution they had made themselves a scourge, until hunted down, wiped out by Sullivan at the orders of Washington, their wild priesthood, sacrilegious to all others of the

Nations, left in smoking embers on crumpled altars.

But it could well be that remnants had survived, that the White Bear, miles and centuries to the west, was a lineal descendant, possessor of the ancient sorcery, eager to launch a new and more terrible crusade.

Poised now at a new Long House, secret and remote, lacking only the discovery of a WHITE priestess, to be discovered by the signs by which she would be marked — hair crimson as flame in the forest, the eyes of the Cat which could see not only by night but the Hidden Things —

A woman to read the signs of ancient rites, to interpret and prophesy —

This new Messiah was proceeding according to tradition, which must not be altered. Weird and wild, unthinkable, it was believable because it had been and was again.

For a while, warfare would be subdued, as fresh recruits gathered, to dance before the Prophet, then, at the Word and the Sign, to sweep like a scourge, east and south, west and north, in ever-widening waves. At the prophesying of the priestess!

And Shenandoah, as much by the ambitious scheming of McQuade as her own natural attributes, was being set apart, ordained, forced to a role not alone hateful but deadly.

For all the heat of afternoon sun, Abbott shivered.

He roused from thoughtful abstraction to

notice that the sun was dimming, the first clouds in weeks beginning to slide across its path. Following so long a spell of good weather, the storm developed swiftly. By nightfall the rain began, and in open country there was no adequate shelter.

It fell drenchingly, long sweeping sheets, drenching the parched land like rivers from the sky. Along with his horse, Montana endured as best he could, conscious of recurring aches from old wounds long healed but unwilling to be forgotten.

Sunshine returned with the new day, but all sign left behind by those who journeyed to meet their prophet had been washed away. He could only keep on, hoping for some trace of the man he sought, guessing as to the others. That he had perhaps guessed wrong, taking a false turn, the long day confirmed, as he failed to find fresh tracks or sign.

More than ever it was an empty land, and ahead — as though set mockingly athwart his path, unwashed by the late storm, agelessly inhospitable, was the desert.

The tired pony jumped in sudden frantic terror, a fraction too slow. There had been no warning, not even an unholy waft of scent to sensitive nostrils. By sheer mischance the cayuse had planted a hoof upon a pair of diamond-backs, and both rattlesnakes had lashed out in equally blind fear, striking simultaneously.

One such bite a horse might survive; Montana

made out the twin sets of punctures on opposite sides of the hock. There was nothing to do but put the tormented horse out of its agony. That the shot might seal his own doom as well was more than likely, but there was no choice.

Chapter Fourteen

Captain Doorley's thoughts were long and somber. Major Connoly, making a surprising recovery, but still wan and pale, had not bothered to send for him the evening before, after Doorley and the men of Charley Company had awakened. Not even to administer what Doorley realized would be a well-merited reprimand. Nor had there been anything of the sort from Montana Abbott, now ranking him, but by report setting off alone on a desperate quest, from which the chances of returning alive were not good.

The Major received him at his request. Doorley fumbled with uncertain fingers at his hat.

Becoming aware of that, of the uneasy shuffling of his feet, he came rigidly to attention, his eyes fixed some six inches above the top of the Major's head.

"I realize that it sounds like an excuse, sir, and I am not trying to do that, or even to explain my conduct. It has been as inexcusable as I fear it was foolish. Have you any orders, sir?"

Connoly studied him with surprise and a touch of sympathy. Some men were slower to learn than others. But at least some did learn, while others never reached that stage. It might still be a long process, but Doorley had the makings of an officer.

"At the moment, I do not," he admitted. "From what I can gather, it appears that Wild Horse and his men have headed north or west, perhaps a little of each. Any immediate risk to this community seems to have lifted. Or would that be a trick, a ruse to throw us off-guard?"

"It might be," Doorley admitted, and considered the notion, then discarded it. "But I would doubt that. I think the braves from a lot of tribes are being called to some meeting, to make medicine — getting set for something a lot bigger, and worse."

"That is my opinion," Connoly agreed, and waited.

"Apparently they've taken Miss O'Shea as a hostage, or — or worse. And Captain Abbott has set out in pursuit — alone!" The big hat was being twisted out of shape, but Doorley was unconscious of that. "I — I am perhaps unfit for such a command, still I request permission, sir, to follow, with as many men as you feel can be spared — perhaps a half of our total force. If and when we succeed in coming up with him, I will of course relinquish command to Captain Abbott."

Major Connoly was conscious of respect, almost of admiration. Doorley was a man, and he was becoming at least a passable officer. What he proposed was wild, bordering on the reckless. but the same notion had been in his own mind, regretfully put aside because there was no one to whom he could reasonably entrust such a command.

Yet there would be no great need for the troopers here, not for some while, and if later, then all was likely to have been lost already. It seemed the one possibility with a chance for success, and this was a time for risks. He stirred impatiently.

"I wish that I was able to ride with you, Captain. Take half the force, as you suggest. And may luck ride with you!"

"Thank you, Sir." Doorley found himself strangely moved. "I realize that we will need it."

"Report to me before you start, in the morning," Connoly added.

"With your leave, Major, we will start within the hour. I hope to be a long way from here by morning."

Shenandoah, riding among a loose caravan of half-naked horsemen, voiced no complaint, recognizing the futility. Jememiah Pedersen groaned but did not weep. "We're alive, though whether that's any reason for thankfulness remains to be seen," she gritted. "But I'd almost as leif be dead as straddling a horse. They are no fit means for locomotion."

"But at least you're with me, and for me that is reason for thanksgiving," Shenandoah reminded. "I would be lost indeed without you."

"But you might be better off without me, and my fool tongue,"Jememiah returned. "Giving you bad advice, to stay on at the ranch, instead of going to the fort along with the rest of them. I thought it was no more than a scare. How wrong can one be?"

"No worse than myself. I thought the same. Besides, there were reasons at the fort, as well as away from it, to stay as far from it as possible."

"The Captain and the sutler!" Jememiah said bitterly. "Sound enough reasons, though some women would account them otherwise. And here comes the one, pestering as usual!"

Both women preserved a forbidding silence as McQuade pushed his horse alongside. Outwardly he gave no indication of uneasiness, though second thoughts had been less reassuring. Against those, and the part he had played, was balanced the realization that Wild Horse would have acted the same in any case, and that there was nothing that he could have done.

Shenandoah's head was bare to the sun, the bonnet jerked loose and flung away, as though to show to everyone the rich flame of her hair. Oddly, the exposed face and throat remained white, neither burning nor tanning in the sun. One more sign, as McQuade realized grimly, that she was a being apart, not as other women.

"You not only look like a goddess, you ride like one," he observed, and drew an expected retort.

"Sight may be deceiving, Mr. McQuade. As with yourself."

Understanding her meaning, McQuade colored. Any possible appreciation for saving her from a worse fate had not been forthcoming. Not only did she hate him, which he could accept, but the certainty that she despised him was harder to take.

"Still, you are slated to be a goddess, a prophetess and priestess," he persisted. "All of which you deserve. Attributes to which you owe your life."

Shenandoah was increasingly curious. This seemed a dream, impossible, carved of fancy. She had been told just enough to increase her bewilderment.

"Are you serious? I'm an ordinary woman, nothing more. This other — what is back of it all?"

"I can't agree that you're just an ordinary woman, Shenandoah. You're much more — especially in the belief of a certain pagan priest and medicine man, who apparently had heard of you quite a while ago, and your extraordinary attributes interested him so much that he wanted to find out a lot more — and apparently succeeded. To the point where he is convinced that you are the one ordained or promised prophetess, provided of course by the Great Spirit of his people, for this special time and occasion. It's not entirely by chance that Wild Horse is taking you to the Great White Bear, less as a hostage than an offering."

"Offering?" Those fantastic eyes widened. "You mean — some sort of sacrifice?"

"I don't think so. I hope not." He was disturbingly sober. "From what I've been able to gather, the Great Bear, the Son of the Sun, is a hereditary priest of an ancient clan of a great Indian federation — and he has the notion that he is a sort of savior or messiah for his people, to lead them out of bondage, to destroy all whites, to sweep them from the land."

Shenandoah could understand that. The elements of leadership were usually based on mystery, on some form of religious observance, on special or supernatural powers.

"But where would I come in?"

"The way I gather it, is that the Bear believes that he is a great leader, one destined to do this work — with the assistance of a priestess who will read the signs and interpret them — and you appear to be the ordained woman, as he is the man. A great pow-wow is in the making. He will

make medicine. He will consult oracles, seek
omens — or maybe you will. You will prophesy,
after which the warriors will be sent out."

Shenandoah shivered. This was fantastic, yet
somehow more and more believable.

"But how could I prophesy? As to being a
priestess, why, that's ridiculous."

"Sounds so to me," McQuade admitted. "But
not to them. And keep this in mind, you'll be
expected to do as commanded. So long as you
do, you'll be safe, honored. You won't have
much choice."

She was beginning to feel frightened.

"But how could I prophesy — even if I wanted
to?"

The sky was darkening, as though with talk of
omens this was a sign. Long calm, to be
succeeded by storm.

"I've no idea," McQuade confessed. Almost he
regretted the part he had played, while realizing
that it would have made no difference. "But
you'll be inducted as a priestess of the Cat
People, a branch of the Eries — and you'd better
cooperate to the best of your ability! As for the
prophesying, I suppose they have drugs,
medicines, and under their influence you might
see visions and dream dreams. At least pretend,
and to the best of your ability. If you don't,
they'll kill you."

137

Chapter Fifteen

Montana awakened to a sense of wrongness, which a quick inspection confirmed to the proportions of disaster. Someone had visited him while he slept, appropriating virtually everything that was loose, then made off with the booty, managing the job so carefully that he had slept through it all.

"But he didn't kill me — which would be easy and safer and natural," he realized, even contrary to redskin nature. Or was that the answer?

It could well be that his life had been spared for the moment so that he should die more slowly, as surely but more painfully, by starvation and thirst. The sun was already bursting above the horizon, a splash of heat in its molten eye. He had reached desert country, in itself a partial answer — the few who prowled these wastes belonged to tribes other than he had encountered, as shadowy and treacherous as other denizens of the wasteland.

A man on foot, without a gun — especially a white man, would soon be in desperate case. His canteen had still sloshed the evening before, still half full. Aside from what it contained, he had been forced by sheer weariness to make a waterless camp, after leaving the dead horse behind.

Faint sign in a sandy patch indicated a moccasined tresspasser, narrower of foot than the average Comanche; in any case, this was not their territory, and one of them, coming upon an enemy, would have been most interested in his scalp.

The thief had missed a couple of items, always carefully wrapped and carried in an inside pocket; small things which could be life-savers in such an extremity, at least in ordinary country. One was a fish-line, with hooks. The other was matches Together they represented food and fire.

The desert stretched bleak and empty. In this section there were none of the giant cacti which might provide food and drink of sorts, enough to sustain life; not even the ground-carpeting prickly pear, also useful in a last extremity. There was only sparse dry grass.

He had a single choice, unless he chose to wait

for death; to keep moving, as long as he could, in the desperate hope of finding water.

An added notch to his belt was a poor substitute for breakfast. As the sun climbed a gradual change came to the country, rendering it slightly more colorful but no more promising. He reached a sparse clump of mesquite, rested briefly in its mockery of shade, then kept going. Eyes aching with the white-hot glare, he could discern no sign which might suggest water.

The heavy rain of a couple of days before had not reached here. Never had he seen a drier land. The shrunken clumps of grass or desert brush seemed long since to have given up the struggle. Rain could green such country almost in a night, filling waterholes, starting sudden streams to a wild coursing. Flowers would erupt out of emptiness, tinting drabness to rainbow hues. Life, dormant but not discouraged, would revitalize itself and restore the land.

Such cycles were as much a part of the desert as the periods of bitter drought. But there was no cloud in the blue bowl of sky.

Some deserts were made up of waves of unending sand, rolling like a sea. This was not that sort. The soil was hot underfoot, but it had the look of quality to please a farmer, almost of richness. On it he had spied no crawling diamond-back, not even a crouching jack-rabbit.

To stop was to admit defeat. But the effort was increasingly hard. The sun was still climbing, close to noon. And still, nothing —

Or was there? Perhaps he'd walked unseeingly. Not far to the side, the flat, empty barrenness was broken by the lift of a small hill. Near its crest, brush made a spreading green clump.

It took a minute to convince himself that it was not an illusion, a mirage or trick of light and vision. Greenery, in such country, was a good indication of water. Whether it might be a spring, breaking to the surface, or deep moisture beyond reach, was to be discovered. Montana moved with a sudden surge of hope.

Grass covered the lower slopes of the hill, dry and brown, but so luxuriantly as to indicate that a considerable seepage had for a while watered not only the clustering brush at the crest but the lower reaches. There were dips and ridges, washed and gashed by sudden floods almost to the proportions of coulees.

Abbott's mouth was gravelly, his knees had been on the verge of buckling as his feet becaue increasingly inclined to stumble. He passed a questing tongue across dry lips, increasing his pace. All at once he could smell, almost taste the water.

It was there, ahead, a considerable pool, cupped near the base of the hill. Its cool glitter was tempting, promising. He started to run.

The whine of a bullet, passing close and at eye level, jerked him to an instinctive crouch. It was followed a moment later by the growl of a pistol. And that, somehow, was more surprising than the rest.

At such a range, few men were marksmen. Panic had perhaps hurried the shot, though it could have been by way of warning. It had come from somewhere on the brushy slope above.

Again, as in the wake of the night prowler, it came as a surprise. There had been no sign of anyone as he walked, no warning until the gun had barked after the manner of a nervous fox. But its purpose and intent, coupled with the timing, was unmistakable. He had been allowed almost to reach the water, then it was denied him. Whether the gunman was the one who had robbed him, or not, by nature they were kin.

He realized that his approach had been watched, probably for a long while. It would have been easy to kill him, but he had been allowed to savor salvation, before being stopped, denied both life or swift death. To perish of heat and thirst, with water almost within reach, was a refinement of cruelty.

"That was a mistake on your part, feller, whoever you are!" Montana voiced his thought in a grim undertone. "It's not my habit to take such treatment lying down!"

The shadow of a grin curled his lips, since he was stretched flat, making himself as inconspiciuous as possible against the chance of another bullet. Lying so, he was probably invisible to the gunman. Carefully, he made a survey.

Nothing moved on the brushy slopes above, the leaves — green rather than shriveled, lacking even a puff of breeze to stir them. The watcher remained comfortably hidden in that shade, secure in what he counted an impregnable position, intent on keeping him just beyond the reach of water.

He could almost smell the water, and the sight of it was added torment. But the warning bullet had been implicit.

From above, the watcher was able to command every approach to the hilltop. He could hold out, in reasonable comfort, for as long as he cared to play such a cat and mouse game. For Abbott there was neither cover nor shade. There would be none, short of darkness. By then, if he could last that long, through the burning heat of afternoon, his enemy would probably put an end to any chance of reaching the water by a second shot.

Apparently the word for war, disseminated from the distant Long House, had reached even here. This fitted the ancient game of torment, directed against any victim hapless enough to come along. It was ingrained practice to torture victims whenever the opportunity was afforded. That applied to men − or women or children − from other tribes, as well as white men, an impersonal hatred, more dreadful on that account. That men of his own race were at times equally guilty made it neither worse nor better.

That might be the answer here, or there could be some more personal reason, with him regarded as an intruder. Should that be so, it might make a difference.

He could shout, demanding an accounting, or explanation, but that would be a waste of breath. The watcher would not betray his position by an answer. However impersonal, the game was deadly.

The heat was intense. Wild creatures would venture to the water hole to drink, but only by night. The absence of bones indicated that the water was good. What he needed was a plan, some way to reach it, short of dying.

A sound came, a groan of agony or torment.

Chapter Sixteen

Startled, Montana peered more carefully, baffled. The groan had seemed to be compounded of pain and the agony of thirst, so it must have come from another victim; certainly not from whoever watched from the shade above.

With sharpened attention he made out the barely visible outline of what could be a man. A slight depression in the ground rendered the other victim all but invisble from where Abbott lay, so that until now he had failed to notice. Closer even to the water than himself, the man was on the far side of the pool, spread-eagled. Without fully seeing, Montana understood. He had been staked out in the sun to endure the added torment of thirst, with water so tantalizingly close, yet hopelessly out of reach.

The other man then would be the original, the chief object of the ordeal, while his captor enjoyed his suffering.

This other victim altered the situation, but not too much. He too, would have to have water, and soon. Otherwise both of them would slowly cook.

Montana glimpsed something else, almost concealed by dry grass, a bit to the side. The end of a bow.

The most reasonable explanation for it was that the other captive, probably an Indian, had lost it and the bow had gone unnoticed, perhaps in a life and death struggle.

Again there was a moaning grown, but it drew no response. Wriggling in a slow and careful crawl, Montana reached, his fingers closing on the tip of the bow, drawing it to him. To his delight, it was strung and ready for use. Always intent on reading sign, he noticed automatically that it was similar to the bows of tribes with which he was familiar, yet with a certain unmistakable difference. That was not only in the workmanship, but in the wood itself — an eastern oak, rather than the western growths beyond the big river.

Even better, three arrows had been dropped when the bow had been lost. War arrows, again similar yet with a subtle distinction of tribe and craftsmanship.

In the hands of its owner, the bow would probably be as deadly as a six gun in his. Montana could claim no such skill with a bow, though he had occasionally practiced, attaining a fair proficiency. The trouble was that he had no target at which to aim, though himself more or less exposed to the watcher above.

He had almost stopped sweating, too drained and dried to perspire, desperately in need of water. Momentarily such discomfort was in the background. There had to be a way. The lives of both the other man and himself depended on finding it.

Then he saw a solution, and began to work back to slightly better cover, unchallenged since he was moving away both from the water and his fellow-victim.

So long as he retreated, he appeared to pose no threat.

Now he was at least partly hidden by the contour of the hill. Forcing himself to studied slowness, less apt to be detected, he pulled a handful of the well-cured grass. Unwrapping his kit, he bit off a length of fish-line, wrapping it around the clustered grass at the middle of an arrow. Fitting the arrow to bowstring, he scratched a match. The grass flared.

The bow required a strong pull to notch and loosen the arrow, trailing smoke as it coursed. Breath in check, he watched its flight. The weighted missile might fall short, or the flame be snuffed in its course. Those chances had to be risked.

The arrow arched, then plunged, to lie smouldering on the slope, hopefully hidden from view of the watcher above by the higher brush. As Montana watched in desperate suspense it seemed to die out; then, at the verge of hope, there was a tongue of flame, a burst of smoke, and the mid-section of hill seemed to explode with a race of fire. The grass was tinder-dry, rich from water, then long curing in the sun. It burnt with frantic eagerness.

Around the base of the slope there was nothing on which it might feeed, but the hill was thickly grassed, then crowned by brush. Earlier in the season, the overflow of springs had kept it well watered. Springs with several outlets were not uncommon.

A seasonal abundance, subsiding with advancing summer, accounted for brush and grass, the still ample supply at the pool.

There was a startled outcry, a wild commotion. Not one, but three men were flushed from their covert, fleeing in a panic of surprise before the racing fire, fanning to each side as it swept up the slope.

They reached the far side, running, badly unsettled by what seemed an impossible turn of events. One steadied at sight of Montana, on his feet, ghostly with the swirl of smoke between. A gun cracked.

It was a long pistol or six-gun range, and by the same token, long bow range, but no worse for one than the other. Fitting another arrow, Montana sent it winging. The gunman dodged, then turned and plunged after his companions.

Panic would keep them going awhile. Such a turning of the tables had shaken them. The brush was burning fiercely, smoke erupting in a crimson-tinted cloud.

Montana reached the water and dropped flat at the edge of the pool, lowering his head, drinking greedily. This spring was cold, sweet as wild honey.

Unsatisfied, he drew back, but to overdo could be disastrous. The other man was probably in worse case. He stared up, understanding beginning to replace the bewilderment on a pinched but strong face, the linaments of a tribe or people of greater power and stature than the trio of desert dwellers who had been sent scurrying. Waves of heat beat almost to where he was pinioned, though scarcely adding to the intense fury of afternoon sun.

Montana struggled unavailingly with the tied, tightly drawn cords which held each hand and foot, then he remembered the fire and grabbed a still burning brand. Presently the flames severed the bonds. He gave the stiffened victim a hand, half-carrying, half-dragging him to the water.

There he drank in turn, but like Montana, with the awareness to check before he was satisfied, plunging instead his head under water, then easing sun-blistered body into the coolness. Montana, after a glance at the diminishing forms of the others, followed his example.

For a while they reveled in the wetness while the stiffened limbs of the captive eased as circulation was restored. By then, the three were gone. For the moment at least they had had enough. Abbott had no doubt that awe and superstition drove them.

No words had been exchanged. They had both been too busy with quenching a prodigious thirst, soaking water through the pores of dry skin, overcoming the burning, enervating effects of the sun. Nothing else was of comparable interest.

But that his companion studied him in turn Montana noticed, a pair of eyes whose vision might rival a hawk's, even as the face was hawk-like, with a matching air of wild pride. Familiar though he was with a number of tribes, not just those which ranged the west but some from east and mid-country, Montana could not place him. Certainly he did not belong to the native peoples, remnants of which ranged this inhospitable bleakness. In such a setting, the plight in which Montana had found him, he seemed as out of place as Montana himself.

Content to allow the silence to flow unbroken, he hoisted himself from the water, stretching restored muscles in sheer enjoyment, then he moved to the base of the hill, now a denuded blackness. The flames were gone, with only a few remaining wisps of smoke near the crest. The ground was scarcely hotter from the roaring sweep of flame than from the long beat of sun.

He searched for a minute among clumps of grass beyond where the fire had reached, coming up with a breech-clout and shirt, apparently stripped from him by his captors and tossed aside. These he donned, then addressed Montana.

"Running Wolf is grateful to his white-skinned brother. It is a service he will not forget."

His English was smooth and fluent, his voice deep and resonant, but Montana scarcely noticed, startled as well as surprised. Here, whether by luck or chance or something planned and beyond understanding, was the man he had come half a thousand miles to find. Running Wolf! For a change, they were both in luck.

Montana nodded, leaving such matters for later. "Why did they stake you?"

The answer came readily enough, only partly comprehensible; words accompanied by an encompassing gesture.

"Cats scratch. And who does the White Bear fear more than the Mohican? Does not the night follow the day?"

153

Chapter Seventeen

"The Great Spirit has guided our steps," Montana returned, with a proper degree of solemnity. "I have been seeking you, running Wolf. I am Montana Abbott."

It was doubtful if his name meant any more to the Mohican than the Sagamore's would have to him, until recently But the other part carried a deep implication, almost a sense of the inevitable.

"Why were they trying to kill you, in such fashion?" Montana asked, though he had little doubt as to the reason.

Running Wolf's face was placid, as though he had already put the event behind him as of no importance. After all, he was a Sagamore, a priest in his own right, and as he accounted it, of the true religion, not one perverted and discredited.

"Coyotes skulk at the fringes of the wolf pack," he said contemptuously. "Those were coyotes, doing the bidding of the Bear, according to their habit and custom. They sought to keep me from the den of the Bear, their secret Long House where fools gather to make medicine — the stinking magic of the Cats!"

For all the placidity of his features he spat the final word.

"Out of fear they serve him, and from the desperation of foolishness he entrusts my destruction to such creatures!

"They came upon me as I slept," he added. "For stealth and craftiness they are unsurpassed. Their weakness is in their desire to torture, rather than in striking swiftly."

Clearly, these lean, half-starved skulkers of the wasteland did not rate high in Running Wolf's estimation. But considering how they had outwitted both the Mohican and himself, he gave them full credit.

In addition to his breech-clout and shirt, Running Wolf's feet were still clad in moccasins. They were sodden but would flex and stretch as they dried with his walking. His bronzed skin was of a lighter hue than those of the desert dwellers. Across a mighty chest, smeared and dimmed by immersion and time, a shadowy stallion reared, the symbol of his name. Aside from that he wore no paint, no other decorations.

His head was shaven, except for a woven scalp-lock. This again contrasted with the poorly tended hair of the coyote pack.

"Truly I was guided to you," Montana repeated. "I too, seek to find this hidden Long House, and the beast who dwells there, this false prophet who styles himself the Great Bear. I have been told that if any man can guide me to that secret place, you are the one."

"That is true." Running Wolf was assured, with no sign of boastfulness. "But why? It is a trail fraught with peril."

"I have two reasons. One is a woman — a woman with green eyes and hair like leaping flames. She is being taken as a gift to the Bear. I must save her."

Again, Running Wolf showed no surprise, "These things I know." He disdained to explain what to him was simple truth, that as a Sagamore, priest of a mighty clan, matters hidden from others were revealed to him in dreams or mystic rites.

"The Bear sent a demand to Wild Horse to bring her! He requires such a woman to be his prophetess, to interpret that which is hidden and speak it aloud! It is because of that that I seek him, so that the evil of his Cat People shall not spread as poison among the innocent. Along with the Bear, it must be destroyed, finally and forever!"

Apparently the presence of the Sagamore, so far from his usual haunts, had become known to the Bear, who would need only one guess as to what brought him on such a hunt. Reason enough to set others to intercept and checkmate him.

Abbott was aware of a growing expectancy, similar to a hunch but more a conviction than a feeling. To the red man, this was both magic and medicine. Whether it was superstition or something more, Montana was not inclined to dismiss it lightly. Judged by results, attacks and bloody forays along a thousand miles of border and spanning centuries, it was only too real.

The sun was finally declining, though the heat was like a blanket across the land. Restored by the water, they set out, Running Wolf taking the lead.

"There is a little Spanish mission, not far away," he explained. "It lies remote, almost forgotten, served by a single priest, his housekeeper and a couple of servants. They minister to red men or white, making no distinction, the mission an oasis in a thirsty land."

Montana did not doubt that the Mohican clung to the ancient beliefs of his own people, but with a tolerant respect for those of other tribes and races. It was only when a once honorable religion was debauched and perverted to the evil purposes of a few leaders that he became infuriated.

Montana glimpsed the mission in the last of the sunset, the whitewashed walls of the church and an adobe gleaming like snow. A cluster of hills rendered the loneliness of the setting less bleak yet somehow more encompassing. A few trees marked the springs which had caused such a site to be selected.

"We will be able to obtain food and such supplies as we must have for our journey," Running Wolf explained. "No horses, I am afraid, but we will do better afoot." His glance rested approvingly on Abbott's long stride, reinvigorated, matching his own. As a cowboy, Montana preferred to ride, but he'd always found his own legs necessary and equal to the demands placed on them.

There had been no discussion as to the journey ahead, no argument. Montana wished to be guided to the Long House, to the White Bear and to Shenandoah. Owing his life to Abbott, Running Wolf was duly appreciative, though clearly he had retained faith in the ultimate power of his own medicine.

Montana had added his second reason, the apprehensions of an old friend who hoped that somehow the Bear might be found and destroyed in his own den, before he could extend the widening war across the land. Montana Abbott, with the guidance of Running Wolf, had seemed the best bet among an assortment of otherwise forlorn hopes. Often a small detachment, sometimes a single man, could penetrate where others were unable to reach, accomplishing the impossible.

Despite grave doubts, Montana had agreed to

.try. The gravity of the situation was only too real. And, deep down, he had admitted the truth to himself. Challenge and adventure were meat and drink to him. He'd lived dangerously too long to be satisfied with a quiet life.

With his purpose, Running Wolf was in sympathy. A friend of the white man, he was as totally an Indian as Wild Horse or White Bear might lay claim to being, having full sympathy with the red man's plight and desire to reclaim an ancient heritage. But he was no fanatical prophet such as he deemed the Bear, nor so foolish as to indulge in wishful but impossible dreaming.

"The Bear is a fool," he said with conviction. "Brave, well-meaning in certain ways, a dreamer — but a fool. His medicine is strong, but evil, therefore it cannot in the long run prevail. In the end he could only lead many to destruction, rendering their plight not better but worse. As the Good Book of the white man proclaims, a blind leader means that those who follow will fall into a pit."

Undoubtedly his judgement was clouded by age-old rivalries, but for all that, Running Wolf was clear-sighted. Like many prior attempts, this effort to unite many tribes and peoples under one banner, to wage triumphal warfare, was foredoomed from the start.

"The hope he raises finds echoes in many hearts," Running Wolf said soberly. "And as an Indian, I understand the dream. The word has spread far, and many tribes, many warriors, are responding, even now on the march, all heading for the Long House. They are drawn to it as by a magnet, hoping, trusting to find in the White Bear the true Son of the Sun, the savior which red men seek, even as white men so long looked for a Messiah.

"I have seen them in the smoke — the warriors who have heeded the call, who are hastening to answer. They would count it an act of valor to slay me, or you — to stop us short of the Long House.

"The pity is that the White Bear is a false prophet, his magic the perverted medicine of the Cat People, spawned in falsehood, steeped in evil. Whatever his intent, he is foredoomed to failure, as are all who put their trust in him. At all costs, for the welfare of all, he must be stopped."

Running Wolf went blithely no more worried by the overwhelming odds against them than Abbott had been when setting out. But the sobering aspect was that the planned uprising was taking on proportions which dwarfed what Montana had expected.

"He has the potential to be a great leader," Running Wolf went on. "I saw him, once. A mystic, well schooled in the ancient-lore but shackled by the thralls of his superstition. He seeks this woman because of her peculiar gifts — one woman among countless thousands, marked with hair which flames and *eyes like a cat's* also with a resolution far above the

161

average. Marked to be a priestess, to prophesy —
a white woman for a red prophet!

"In such superstition lie the thralls which bind
him and doom his cause to failure. If he was to
strike now, leading boldly, he might go far. But
to observe every rite of his priesthood, moving
only when the auguries add to propitious signs —
they cumber with too great a weight, slow his
warriors from running to creeping and foredoom
all to failure!"

Montana listened with increasing wonder and
respect. What Running Wolf was saying was that
a leader who hoped to succeed must have
imagination, casting aside superstition and ancient
thralldom, striking siwftly and boldly.

Days or weeks would be lost in gathering at
the remote Long House, time enough for doubt
and apprehension, for dissension to erupt among
tribes long hostile, hard to hold in any sort of
confederation. Time for dispatching more men in
blue, to mount a counter-blow.

Chapter Eighteen

Blackjack McQuade was increasingly exhilarated. Always he had been a primitive man, impatient of restraint. The realization that he had been born into an environment too civilized and circumscribed for his potential was growing with each mile into the unknown. This was wild country and he was among men as primitive as himself.

Far from being the loser, in the loss of that wagon with its rifles, he had discovered a greater potential and more to his liking.

It had been his idea, or at least his suggestion, to swoop down and grab Shenandoah, to take the flame-haired woman as a gift to this new Messiah.

Since the Bear sought a priestess, and so much would hinge on her, he should be appreciative.

It was true that Shenandoah and Jememiah Pedersen journeyed as captives, under the protection of Wild Horse; but he was one of the escort, accepted as a leader of an increasingly motley horde, as others joined with them. On McQuade's tongue was a foretaste of power.

Whites would term him renegade, but a red man was inherently broader in viewpoint and acceptance. Many white men had become Indian, some through capture, by training and inclination; others, like himself, turning their talents for leadership against their own kind, accepted for what they were.

Once he had delivered Shenandoah to the White Bear, the Prophet would need such a lieutenant as himself.

That Shenandoah scorned and hated him with increasing bitterness he shrugged aside. The trail to the Long House was long, and an ironical twist was that for much of the journey, he knew this country probably better than any other white man, better than most Indians; as a guide he was proving invaluable. Beyond the Long House the trail would broaden.

The little missioner received them hospitably, greeting Running Wolf as a friend. He was sorry that they could tarry no longer than a night, regretful that he could supply them with so little which they required. But what he was able to provide was essential.

With bow and arrows, matches, fishline and hooks, Running Wolf saw no need for more, though he was pleased with a blanket against nights which would grow increasingly chill. They traveled steadily until mid-day, then rested until the sun dipped. By then they were in hill country, the desert behind. Their trend, Montana noted, was north by east.

Running Wolf, having accepted him as a friend, talked freely along most lines. He had never seen the Long House, patterned after the long houses which the Six Nations had used centuries before, in country beyond the lakes and bordering the eastern seaboard. The decimation and scattering of the peoples due to war and the continued encroachments of the white men had left the long houses as little more than a memory.

Now the White Bear had sought a new but equally remote location, an all but inacessible spot for building a new Long House; it was to be both symbol and headquarters, as difficult to reach as the original headquarters.

With it nearing completion, he had gone on to the next step, dispatching runners, summoning tribes from near and far to a great council, a making of medicine; that the purpose was war required no explanation or elaboration.

The unexpected rising of Wild Horse, quickening the pace as it did the imagination, had hastened and was crystallizing the movement.

"Wild Horse would have done better to press

his own war hard and fast," Running Wolf observed. "He has a gift for leadership, where it counts — in the field. A priest or a prophet may not be a warrior," he added cryptically.

The Long House was somewhere in mountain country, a land as high as it was remote. The Bear had considered such trappings ncessary to the proper launching of his movement, a place where an army could gather.

Almost at once it became apparent that others than themselves were on the march, with a common destination. The promised magic, powerful medicine which would cause all warriors to prevail against the common enemy, the excitement of a leader sent by the Great Spirit — the combination was drawing men by ones and twos, also by dozens and scores. Most were on foot but some had horses.

For all the purposefulness of their movement, they followed the stealth of tradition, leaving little sign, gliding like shadows, virtually invisible. A few times, Running Wolf pointed out signs, which eyes less skilled would have missed. Once he halted to stare, raising an arm to indicate distant figures in a file across an open meadow.

In a land so vast the others were few, but a hazard. Should any guess that Running Wolf was a Mohican, a Sagamore of the Magic Clan, they would go to any lengths to kill him. That Abbott, as a white man, added to the risk was beyond question but Running Wolf shrugged it aside.

"You saved me from an increasingly unpleasant experience," he reminded. "It was ordained that we go together. We have work at the Long House."

On the third afternoon, as they rested during the hottest part of the day, Running Wolf, having procured certain berries and other stains from the woods about them, painted himself, squatting crosslegged. He began with his face, proceeding to shoulders, then arms and chest.

Montana watched with interest as he applied the emblems of war and death — reds, yellows, black, all pointed with a garish white. These were the insignia of a chieftan, a proven warrior, also, Abbott suspected, of priest and Sagamore. Since an encounter might be forced on them at any time, Running Wolf deemed it proper to be ready.

Montana's thoughts strayed to Shenandoah. Increasingly he regretted not getting to the ranch ahead of the others, though he had been taken under arrest to the post, and by then it had probably already been too late.

Her unusual beauty had been her undoing, though it could also be her protection. But only for a while. High spirited, she might defy the Bear as she had scorned Doorley and McQuade. Even if she cooperated to the best of her ability, that could be no guarantee of safety. It was increasingly necessary to reach the Long House.

Travel even by night was increasingly

hazardous. Running Horse knew where he wanted to go but there was a wide difference between a general knowledge and finding a way, over and through country increasingly rough and difficult. More than once they were forced to turn back, to find a passable route. That others were having as much trouble was evident.

For the others, there would be guides, acolytes despatched by the Bear to assist strangers when they were at fault. The measure of their acceptance of the Bear as a leader and prophet was attested by the devotion of such virtual slaves, as they were initiated into ancient and secret rites. There was nothing surprising in their willingness, even eagerness for such roles. Indians delighted in secret societies, rituals which tested their stamina and resolution to the utmost, proving themselves as braves before gaining glory as warriors.

Acolytes of such a priesthood would be trained to many duties, believing themselves the possessors of mystic powers bestowed upon them partly by the Son of the Sun, partly through the favor of the beasts they emulated. Running Wolf checked suddenly, at the edge of a stream. An incautious footprint showed in the sand at the water's edge, a mark so faint and insidious that Abbott would have passed it by, with no more at most than an apprehensive glance for the creature which had made it.

The print was of a bear's hind foot.

"Acolyte," Running Wolf spat, glaring about,

and Montana felt his scalp prickle. Not a bear, but another sort of beast in bear's skin, wearing it despite the heat and discomfort; a creature to sniff out alien scents, working in the certainty that he was endowed not only with a bear's powers and instincts, but its fighting ability.

If there was one there would be others — creatures of forest and field, prowlers of darkness, rarely glimpsed, unlikely to be recognized even if seen. These were the outward symbols of the forbidden religion which honest warriors of the Nations had despised even as they shuddered, revived again by a man in the guise of a prophet.

Provided with such trappings of power and mystery, it was no wonder that the chosen ones would respond eagerly.

Runnings Wolf's fingers on his arm stayed Montana as he was about to rise amid a dense cluster of reeds and grasses alongside the creek. They waited. Though schooled to such things on more than one occasion, Abbott marveled at the restraint of his companion in the midst of increasing discomfort. Small flies sought them out, mosquitoes came with the approach of evening. The small breeze which had afforded a measure of relief died away.

Thirst increased the discomfort, with water rippling past only a few feet away, but out of reach. Above its surge and ripple, Montana became conscious of other sounds, small stirrings which might be made by rabbit or mink, wolf or

169

weasel, but were not. Beyond the twitch of a distant bush he could make out nothing. From sensing danger, it became a conviction that the woods and brush were peopled with others who also waited and watched, creatures who tested the air, suspicious, deadly in their alertness.

Grim with determination to hold out as long as his companion, who would scoff and keep moving at ordinary danger, he managed the wait as darkness came down. Finally, after a further interminable delay, the Sagamore's hand on his arm was a signal and they moved, reaching the water.

The moon would soon be up, but now a scatter of distant stars gave the only light. The creek ran cold and dark. To Montana's surprise, Running Wolf remained in the water, following the creek. They moved carefully, placing each foot without drip or swirl, careful of slippery stones or tripping.

The sense of danger was stronger, as though an emanation was given off by hidden creatures. That the sachem smelled it also, Abbott could not doubt. Either they had penetrated into the midst of enemies, or the acolytes, spies of the Bear, had picked up their scent but so far were unable to find them. With as eerie an instinct as the creatures they emulated, they were eager, prowling.

They made a long stone's throw, rounding a bend of the creek. A slurry of rapids ended in a long deep pool, the light like a knife-cut down the center. Evergreens on the shores formed a canopy and Abbott was reminded of the long houses, of secret and bloody rites. Then Running Wolf's hand was on his arm, impelling him down, ever deeper, until the water closed over both of them.

Starved for air, he raised his head cautiously, in time to hear a faint splash which might have been a beaver, but was not. Ripples spanned the pool. Something crested the water, moving, no longer creating even a stir. It had the seeming of a beaver, only this was larger, pausing as though to scent the air, to scan the shores. Montana felt a shiver despite himself, but with no sense of relief as he made out the wolf's head. A wolf would not be in the water —

A second creature lurked at the far edge, outlined as the rising moon silvered the water; vacant eyes looked sightless, but behind them was a terrible, question intensity. Running Wolf was gone from beside him, in matching silence.

The wolf's head was working closer. Abbott tensed, then there was a small swirl, the head was gone, and the water churned to wild threshing. A darker stain rippled at the surface. Running Wolf's head emerged, his hand beckoned.

Here the water was too deep for wading. Montana swam, and something reached and clutched from underneath, slippery as a fish, monstrous, but with raking claws at the end of a hairy arm.

Chapter Nineteen

The absence of sound rendered the attack doubly uncanny, but Abbott's nerves were strung for action. Twisting away, he lunged in turn, grabbing. His arms closed around a hairy waist, claws scratching frantically but ineffectually. The terror of the unknown, turned against itself, was in his antagonist. Montana's feet found solid bottom, and he twisted, releasing his grip with one hand, ducking under, closing his fingers on a stone.

There was a choked, bubbling scream as he hammered, then the wildly squirming thing in his grip went limp, and was lost and gone. All at once the pool seemed empty.

Running Wolf whispered from alongside as he reached the shore. The rocky bottom extended outward, forming a narrow beach. Beyond it was a litter of pine needles.

The water had been cold, but only back in the shade of the evergreens, the night air warm about them, did Montana discover that he was shaking. It was easy to understand the horror and aversion which others of the Six Nations had felt for the Eeries from along the lake, those called the Cat People.

For nearly an hour they moved steadily but cautiously, before the Sagamore relaxed. The recollection of the pool, of those silent stalkers who had taken to it, was slow to go away. That their destination, the half-mystical Long House, was still distant, Montana knew, but the power of its priest held an ever longer reach.

Several aspects were becoming clear. Though proclaiming that he was a messiah, a savior of his people, the White Bear was cautious, undoubtedly fearful, hiding away as much for his own protection as for the effect of the unknown. It was not a fear of the scattered whites, across a couple of states or territories, or even of the soldiers who, rousing to the threat, would be mustering, moving against the Bear's gathering hordes.

The White Bear's fear centered on a rival priest, on the inheritor of the ancient, undying emnity between rival religions. Fear of the man who walked at his side, who had become companion and friend.

Unquestionably the Bear had learned of Running Wolf's counterhunt, of his lone but relentless quest, to reach the Long House and an accounting long overdue. The White Bear's fear was not alone for the physical prowess of Running Wolf as a warrior, but for the fearsome powers of a rival priest.

Knowing that Running Wolf was on his trail, the Bear had sought to destroy him in the desert, enlisting the aid of allies. That attempt had failed, but the acolytes had picked up the trail, deep in this wilderness, and were as savagely determined.

Their quality as scouts and warriors, even without the added fearsomeness of the guise in which they went, had been amply demonstrated.

They rested, each standing watch while the other slept, a mark of respect accorded only major foes. Remembering how both of them had come to grief while they slept, Montana did not protest. One mistake was enough. A second could well prove fatal.

Montana pulled fish from another stream as the dawn lightened the east and was not surprised to find Running Wolf ready with a small, smokeless fire for roasting them. With the endless rigors of the trail, both hungered for red meat, but the risk was too great.

"How much farther?" Montana asked, and stripped the salmon-colored meat neatly from the framework of whitened bones.

"Several days, still," Running Wolf admitted and lifted his head as if to test the air. "Had we horses — as do some others — but with them we might blunder into a snare," he added regretfully. "Otherwise we would help ourselves."

Listening, Abbott became aware of a faint but familiar sound — the plodding hoof-strokes of horses. Among the hills it was impossible to determine accurately the direction, but they were not far off.

Montana's thoughts went to Shenandoah. She would of course have been given a horse to ride. With added speed, undoubtedly she would already have reached the Long House. The rising sun seemed dimmer, the day almost cold.

Shenandoah's mouth twisted; her lips, soft as the petals of the wild roses which only weeks before had spangled the streams, red as their fruit now flaunting through leafy clusters, showed scorn for herself.

"A priestess!" she thought. "Me! And prophetess! That means vision, foresight. If only I had possessed even a little!"

So short a while before, she had been convinced that talk of Indian trouble would be no more than that, that the threat must soon pass. Even when others had taken fright, she had been sure that with her crew any possible dangers could be weathered at the ranch.

There might be added risk, even danger for herself, for wildly improbable reasons, had not occurred to her. What had she to do with signs and omens, even if her hair was red? How those could mark her as ordained to be a priestess of a pagan cult, to prophesy for a savage priest, had been too fanciful to waste a second thought upon.

Even then it could not have happened, except for the absence of all but one of her crew, rounding up the scattered herd — that, coupled with the despicable trickery of Blackjack McQuade —

The curl of her lip changed to scorn at the depths to which he had descended. Looking from the kitchen doorway, she had seen a man, weaving and staggering as he approached the house, falling, struggling on, falling again.

The third time he had lain unmoving, as though badly hurt, perhaps dying. Conditions being as they were, that could easily be so. She could not leave anyone to perish, within sight of her help.

Only as she and Jememiah had reached him had she had a look at his face, as he roused and turned, leering triumphantly. McQuade. By then, Wild Horse's braves had been upon them.

Little by little she had heard enough to piece together where they were being taken, and why. Not as ordinary captives, though whether that was a lesser or a greater horror she was far from certain. Respect, even courtesy, was accorded her, extending to Jememiah as her companion. Respect tinged by awe, a measure of fear.

Already, in the eyes of her abductors, of others who came in contact with them along the trail, she was a priestess, somehow allied with the White Bear, the Red Priest.

Just what that might imply, or how fearsome, she could only guess, but it was not reassuring. A journey which under other conditions would have been a delight, adventurously probing into a wildly beautiful country, had lost all power to charm. War scented the air, like the mists and smokes of autumn. It was not alone in the appearance, the mein of Wild Horse's warriors, but something as clearly to be sensed as the winter which would tread hard on the heels of Indian Summer, even the flaming leaves portents of savagery . . .

The wilderness around them grew deeper, darker, its very breath more hostile. The sight of more warriors, occasionally crossing their path or even traveling awhile with them, men with painted faces, chests and arms, braves from differing tribes, some of whom normally were hostile — those were frightening enough. Though not nearly so much as rare glimpses of creatures which skulked, impossible beings, fantasies out of a nightmare. A brown bear, erect on its hind legs — and walking, a bow and arrow in its paws! A pack of wolves, crouching, sniffing, noses to the wind. And at the rim of a patch of brush, the ears of a puma.

A horse, a horned bull, a creature deserving of itself to be termed a devil — Indian devil of myth and dreadful reality, the wolverine.

A friendly brave, respectful though unwilling, answered her question in part; these were scouts, guides, priests of a lower rank; creatures who served the Bear.

In her heart she had clung to what she realized was no more than a foolish hope, that Abbott would find a way to follow. There was something about him, not alone his reputation —

One relief came with increasing miles and passing days. McQuade no longer rode with Wild Horse or alongside. As zealous as any Indian and as savage, his talent for leadership had been recognized. Someone had seen to it that he was placed at the head of a motley group who in outward seeming were little different from the others heading for a common rendezvous. Even their skins, burnt by sun, greased and painted, were scarcely lighter. Renegades, white men who made so desperate a cause their own. Cast out by their own society, with nowhere else to go. Outlaws, as much wolf's-heads as the skulking acolytes. Full a score. A fitting command for such a man as McQuade.

Priestess, to a savage pagan! Prophetess, for a perverted religion! The white teeth closed painfully on the red lip beneath.

Chapter Twenty

Doorley set a steady pace, less fast than once had been his custom, but more considerate of men and horses and to his astonishment covering more ground in a day. He was silent for the most part, more subdued. Lieutenant Van Dyke, jogging alongside, was first astonished, finally amazed. This was a new Doorley, one who listened to his scouts and guides, who asked advice and acted upon it.

And who led them, few doubted, to their death.

Not alone the men but the scouts rode with doubt, for they followed no known trail, to no certain destination. But the mystical Long House must be somewhere, and gradually their way was made easier by the passage of others, almost certainly bound for the common goal; strangers like themselves to the land, unusual riders on an uncanny pilgrimage. Almost all, by the sign, were Indians, who oddly did not quarrel or fight each other, but would not be adverse to the taking of scalps along the way. Most moved with skill and stealth but some were not at home in such a land. A trail of sorts was being laid.

Somehow it was uncanny, strange to the point of disbelief. The gathering of peoples, the making of an army. Indians, with few exceptions, had never responded well to such calls. Now they were putting aside quarrels, forgetting ancient animosities in a common purpose. The magic of a warrior, a priest of medicine and magic. How long such union might endure belonged to the future, but for the present it was amazing, frightening.

"If this White Bear can keep 'em together — get them to fight together, he stands a damn good chance of sweeping out us whites same as a bunch of cats in a mouse nest," an old-timer observed. "He'd sure enough have the man-power, and all of them good fighters. But the rub of any army comes when they have to hang together, to fight together. Indians just won't do that."

That last assertion was Doorley's article of faith. He had nothing else on which to pin it.

Surprise came with a sudden onset, warriors striking from ambush. Doorley had been expecting something of the sort, knowing that their presence, their every move was known and watched. He had taken such precautions as were possible, but this was country perfect for such tactics. Even had he been aware, it would have been impossible to guard against the attack. To go forward was to ride into the trap. To turn back would have insured pursuit, while other warriors struck from either side as well as ahead — as they were doing.

There was a new spirit in the men of A Company, coupled with the certainty of death if they faltered. they gained the respect of the enemy, the admiration of their officers, and Lieutenant Van Dyke succeeded, after an interval, in forcing a way through the trap, to safety. Some few dead remained behind, but more of those wore paint than uniforms.

A Company suffered what once would have been no loss, but now ranked as a disaster. A prisoner taken, alive. Their captain.

Dazed from the glancing blow of a tomahawk, forced along by a swarm of captors, Doorley was scarcely aware of either his plight or his surroundings, while they hurried ever deeper into an unfriendly wilderness. Only sometime after night came down did they halt. Tied hand and foot and thrown to the side as contemptuously as an old sack, he was forgotten or mercifully ignored for much of the night. The fight had been bitter while it lasted, more battering to both sides than they had counted on. Even the victors

183

were too tired for anything unnecessary, even sport.

Cramped and uncomfortable, increasingly hungry and thirsty, Doorley managed to get just enough sleep to clear his head and make him fully aware of his plight. There could be no hope of rescue, he realized, in a land swarming with enemies. He was alive, but it would have been better had the axe struck. They would have but one purpose in keeping him alive, this long.

Daylight awakened them, and now there was a fresh mood — not quite jovial, though with a hint of rough humor, an anticipatory spitefulness. For the present they had lost the desire to hasten to reach the Long House. That could wait.

There was an abundance of game, and the hunters brought in more than was needed. Presently the tang of wood smoke mingled with savory odors of roasting flesh. Animals were turned on spits above the flames. Fish were soon ready and devoured, no more than a whet to ravenous appetites. They tore then at half-cooked, half-raw flesh. Doorley squirmed at the fragrance.

In the middle of the feast, a brave, hideously painted in maroons and greens, jumped to his feet and crossed to where Doorley lay, clutching a half-gnawed bone. He tendered it under Doorley's nose, then, as with sudden understanding, snatched a knife and cut the thongs which held Doorley's wrists and ankles.

The relief, after long cramping, was offset by

pain as the flow of blood resumed. Doorley's teeth cut his lower lip as he kept from crying out, the taste of blood salt and bitter. Again the bone was tendered. He reached dazedly, to have it jerked away, amid a jibing chorus of kicks and laughter.

The torment of thirst had been sharpened by the ripple of water close by and with daylight it was visible. Apparently unnoticed as the others ate wolfishly, Doorley started to crawl. He felt a small hope, nearing the water, then was caught and dragged back as he was at the point of lowering his head to drink.

As though on signal, taunts and blows increased. The words were meaningless, but their sense was clear enough. Had there been any doubt of their ultimate intentions, those were dissipated as some set about ominous preparations, in the middle of the little, natural clearing.

Up to then, the grassy meadow, surrounded by giant evergreens, had been almost a small paradise. Now it was to become a place of execution. Digging a hole was slow and difficult, even with sticks and war axes, scooping out the dirty by hand. This war party obviously did not belong to the Six Nations or any of their descendants, lacking anything in the line of agricultural tools or skill at using them. But the hole for the stake was gradually deepened.

Sitting, back to the trunk of a big tree, Doorley watched the preparations. The stake

185

would be implanted, wood piled about its base as he was tied, jointly with it to become a torch. But they were in no hurry. Half of the pleasure of such a ritual lay in anticipation, both for the victim and the onlookers. Haste, diluting both, would to some extent defeat the purpose.

More than once in recent days, Doorley had wondered how he might meet such a situation, if it were forced upon him. Always he had had a sick sense of doubt. He had proven to his own satisfaction a headlong courage in the heat of battle, but such a death was not the same. He reminded himself that it could hardly be worse than the anticipation, which they understood to a nicety. But his flesh shrank.

He held his face impassive, as though he was one of the spectators, steeling himself not to flinch from kicks, or the sudden whipping strokes of knife or tomahawk, checked so that they barely scraped eyelashes or throat. Several times they brought water, to jerk it back just short of his mouth.

Pride and resignation kept him from collapse. Then soul and body seemed to sicken, as several braves staggered into the clearing, throwing down a sizeable trunk of dead tree which would serve as the stake.

Word of what impended was spreading. Others were arriving, stopping to enjoy the spectacle. Doorley stiffened incredulously as a file of horsemen came, bridles jangling to the accompanying creak of saddle leather. It was the saddles which assured him that they were white men, for in nearly every other aspect they outshone the savages.

Only McQuade, at their head, was unmistakable. He pulled to a stop, staring down, a slow smile twisting the corners of his mouth. Doorley was torn by conflicting impulses, to spit or jeer, showing his contempt for the turncoat. But another impulse was as hot throughout him as when circulation had started its return through cramped arms and legs. With it came the certainty that he was a coward, and that he did not even care.

"So," McQuade murmured. "I'd heard that a bunch of the boys had found themselves a plaything — but that it might be you had not entered my mind."

"It's what they call the fortunes of war." Doorley managed a shrug. "It is a strange meeting."

"Strange indeed." Triumph reddened McQuade's eyes. At the fort they had outwardly passed as friends, even when rivalry stood between. McQuade was mockingly sympathetic.

"It's sorry I am to see you in such plight, Captain Doorley. A brave end to a soldier's career, but a bad one."

"The end?" Doorley repeated. "We are white men," he reminded, and forced the words to run without emotion. "And white men stand together."

"I sympathize with you," McQuade reiterated.

"But as you may have noticed, this is Indian country. They brook no interference at any time, least of all now. Even to suggest what you are asking would be tempting a like fate."

"Yet a MAN might try," Doorley reminded, and his hands moved in swift gesture. From their days at the fort he had learned that they were brothers of an order as ancient as it was honorable.

McQuade's eyes dilated, then narrowed, even as his face went from pale to crimson.

"Do you think to work on my sympathy with that?" he demanded. "I could do nothing, even if I would. And I am not a fool!"

"And you wouldn't, if you could," Doorley flung back, but McQuade was riding on, as though with an urgent memory of something up ahead.

Chapter Twenty-one

Montana roused to sudden attack, an exultantly shouted war whoop ringing in his ears, but voiced an instant too soon; simultaneous with it was the chukking of a hard-flung tomahawk, burying itself where his head had lain a moment before. His antagonist's aim had been partly spoiled by the springing leap of Running Wolf, straight at the man so suddenly weaponless.

Enemies had crept close while they slept, but their surety of success had been too soon voiced; and the Sagamore, Abbott had discovered, slept as lightly as the Cats he abhorred.

Running Wolf was in hot pursuit, running in great bounds like a hound, but a second creature burst from the gloom, hurling itself upon Montana before he could gain his feet, wrestling savagely, trying to pin his arms, to strike with a dagger-pointed blade. In the beginning dawn Abbott was conscious of a black wolf's head, rearing above a ghastly white underlay spread across a broad chest, of skin oiled and slippery, writhing away from his grasp. The point of the knife poised above his throat, but the stroke stayed helplessly as his fingers twisted on the wrist. Lips writhed back from snarling teeth in a matching snap of bone.

The knife scuffed beneath their feet as Montana exerted his strength, flinging the brave into a patch of brush. But by the time he could snatch the lost dagger and leap for a finish a crashing sound marked flight.

It was as much luck as skill which kept him alive through the day. Between them, he and Running Wolf had accounted for an equal pair, but there were others, swarming as invisibly yet insistently as the little black flies, their bite a harbinger of winter. For all its stealth, the hunt was relentless. Half a dozen times, Abbott glimpsed nightmare creatures who sniffed the air but, beyond that initial whoop, ran silent.

Night was slow in coming, but the longest day has its end. Montana missed the strength and sureness of Running Wolf. He could only guess as to how widely they were separated.

Here in mountain country fall was on the march, the night air blowing chill. A small dividend was a handful of ripening berries, still with a puckery taste of greenness, a scant sop to hunger.

The blacker part of the night provided reasonable security, and he risked a brief sleep, coming awake as planned with the rising of the moon.

None too soon. Shadowing away from the spot where he had lain, he discovered a wolf which crept, paused, sniffed at the warmth left by his body, and was suddenly wary; the incautious snapping of a dry stick revealed a puma, the tawny head thrust forward, above the running legs of a man.

Had it been a matter of choice, the next few hours of half light were too close a repetition of the day. The hunt continued, relentless, determined. His realization that with daylight they could hardly fail to close in did not make for relaxation.

He came upon what was almost a trail; other men had clearly passed, not long before. A great tree leaned outward, the first branches well above his head. With an upward leap bettering his best, Montana closed his fingers over an outreaching limb, clung, then pulled himself up. Climbing a score of feet, he found a snug, almost comfortable perch between the crotch of massive limb and the trunk of the tree.

Again, it was none too soon. Stir and movement warned that others were following the trail, more open than those who had hunted him, grown careless from weariness. Shadows dimmed the space below, but he discovered with dismay that the newcomers were availing themselves of the open ground for a camp, intent on remaining for what was left of the night.

Grimly, Montana took stock. He still had bow and arrows, hooks and fish line, a few matches. Little enough, as the growing day revealed a sight which dismayed, then sickened him with realization. This party had a captive, a white man. It was some while before he could obtain a good enough look to be sure that the prisoner was Doorley. With that came the added certainty that he had a prime seat from which to watch a man's death by burning.

Their intent became increasingly clear as the day dragged and the hole was dug. The stake was half-dragged, half-carried into view, dropped thuddingly upright, and firmly set.

One thing alone was good. Intent on their victim and the business at hand, none thought to look for enemies overhead. The trunk and limb, with more branches below, afforded a reasonable screen.

That he would be compelled to endure thirst and hunger and an increasingly cramped position through the day was mitigated only a little by the similar yet worse torment for Doorley. Abbott's respect, which had grown on the last day or so of their association, sharpened to admiration. Doorley played a man's part.

Montana pondered their positions, bitterness

like heartburn in throat and chest. Death in battle might be faced with reasonable fortitude, but in the delayed torment of flame and choking smoke it was as devilish a torture as such men could devise; no worse, on balance, than had crept upon Running Wolf, spread-eagled to the baking torment of sun and insects, yet certainly no better.

He had been able to save the Sagamore from that, and now he was in a position to cut short Doorley's suffering. It could be managed with an arrow, driven straight and hard; no murder, that, but mercy. Montana had no doubt of his ability to send an arrow where he aimed, at such direct range.

The problem was what must follow hard upon its speeding. Doorley's captors would be taken aback, not understanding in the first moments of shocked surprise, but recovering quickly as they saw the arrow and its direction of flight.

He might be able to hold them off for a short while, as long as his arrows lasted. Then they would shoot him down in turn, or worse, drag him to occupy the position vacated by Doorley, to roast in his stead.

Such alternatives left him more hollow at the pit of the stomach. To sit idly and watch Doorley die, surviving because inaction was his only way of life —

What he would do, Montana was not sure. Before long, he would have to decide, by acting — or failing to act.

He strained with interest, to catch what was said between Doorley and McQuade, and understood. Both men belonged to a secret order, one with its beginnings rooted in antiquity. Only honorable men were supposed to be allowed in membership, but misfits crept in. Doorley had made a signal of distress, by which a fellow was required in honor to respond.

That Doorley resorted to it, to such a man and under such conditions, was a measure of his desperation, fear like fire in heart and mind.

McQuade's refusal, however he could fail to guess its effect, increased the pressure on himself to aid when time impelled, in the one way possible. Sweating, Abbott was cold.

More wayfarers were arriving, entering the clearing, men on foot rather than horses, Indians instead of renegades. A few, coming up quickly, straddled wiry Indian ponies. One was Wild Horse.

The chief halted, staring down with expressionless face. At McQuade's refusal, Doorley had slumped, closing his eyes. Now, as though conscious of that look, he opened them, staring without expression. The chief revealed his training among white men.

"I am sorry to see you here, Captain Doorley. It had not occurred to me that you might be the captive."

Doorley's glance quickened. Following past encounters, such an expression on Wild Horse's part was a handsome tribute. Doorley recalled something which he had heard about this red man who for a time had walked in the ways of the white.

"You show more sympathy than the sutler," he returned and again, swift and puzzling to such other eyes as watched, he repeated the gesture of distress.

Wild Horse's eyes contracted. He was a warrior, and a chief. According to his own code, he fought honorably. He yielded to no white man in his recognition of a gentleman.

"What could I do, even if I wished?" he asked. "These who hold you — they are not my people, nor would they recognize my authority. Even to attempt to help you — "

His shrug was eloquent. Doorley sank back.

"At least, you are honorable in intent," he retorted. "I appreciate that."

The eyes of the chief seemed to glaze. He had made excuses, and he was not a man to indulge in apology. Abruptly he took his decision. This man was an enemy, but Wild Horse had once pledged his honor. He swung on the others who were grouped about, watching between rage and unease.

"This man is under my protection," he said in English. "I do not ask your permission. I, Wild Horse, take him. Let no man harm him, short of my return."

Then he spoke in a dialect unintelligible to Abbott, but to those who held the prisoner. They listened sullenly, then protested, but Wild Horse was insistent. Presently he went on, his followers at his heels. His final words were a grim reminder that he would be back, and at need demand an accounting.

Doorley sat a little straighter, his back to the tree trunk, with a sudden hope. His captors were angry, but impressed and uncertain. Wild Horse was known and respected. What he promised he would do.

The impasse did not last long. Clearly, someone carried the word to McQuade, not too far ahead. Within half an hour he was back, his painted horde galloping at his heels. Power had come to him as it had to Doorley, and he too found it a heady brew. Wild Horse had been an ally but never a friend, a bitter word had passed between them.

"To hell with Wild Horse," he growled, and the malignancy of the man showed naked. "Since I refused this dog protection, who is he to give it? I command here, by order of the Bear. Take him."

One of his men interpreted, repeating the order for the benefit of the Indians. Instantly they were exultant, twice eager after the uncertainty. Doorley was jerked to his feet and dragged across to the stake. They tied him in place with ropes passed around it and under his arms. His wrists were bound separately.

A great pile of dry wood, already collected, was piled about his feet. McQuade met his glance with a grim smile.

"You had the poor judgement, the temerity, to put yourself in opposition to me from the start, Doorley, thinking to have such a woman as Shenandoah, when I aspired to her! And now you try to go over my head, as though I would permit you to live! I've no doubt you'll fry well. My only regret is that I can't spare the time to watch. But these others will attend to your every need, here at the gates of hell. So to their mercies I leave you."

Chapter Twenty-two

Even with a good horse to ride, treated respectfully and with a sense of awe, Shenandoah had found the trail long and tiring. When finally a valley opened up ahead, seeming to extend a welcoming atmosphere, there was almost an aspect of homecoming. Shenandoah looked about with lively interest.

They had followed rough ways, winding among hills which merged into mountains, leaving even the suggestion of civilization behind. The original Long House had been remote and hard to reach, and the Bear, emulating that pattern, had found another site which matched.

It was a place of natural beauty, flanked by

mountains, shrouded by forest, unspoiled. That despite changes and preparations over a period of months, perhaps years. Following ancient custom, squaws had toiled, assisted however unwillingly by acolytes and even braves, turning under the grass of open meadows, planting crops. In this sheltered spot where the sun reached warmly, in virgin soil rich with the cumulus of centuries, gardens flourished. Corn stood high, ears at the milk. Pumpkins and some other crops, long the mainstay of their people, added a promise of golden harvest.

The home-like aspect was increased by a number of small cabins at the rim of the big meadow, against a sheath of trees. Shenandoah could make out nothing which might be the Long House, but she guessed that it would be in some even more hidden vale.

A jarring, almost alien note was intruding with the arrival of strangers, the vanguard of the tribes who were responding to the summons to gather to make medicine, to unite in a common purpose and then, pursuing it, sweep as a conquering horde across the land. Tepees had sprung up; men and horses ranged alongside or even trespassed upon the gardens. Shenandoah made out three separate camps, each clearly from a different tribe, warily neutral on this ground but with ancient hostilities barely in check.

The two white women were given a cabin, their needs provided by squaws who seemed unmoved by the mounting excitement which

200

pervaded the gathering. That was understandable. Drudgery was their life, increased by the added demands of such an influx. Others might join in the festivities, the dances, rites and making of medicine, afterward to go forth to conquer. None of that affected them. They would stay on.

The maidens were different, young, proud, comely, clearly chosen to serve the White Bear, from among the many. Seven were assigned to attend the Prophetess, respectful but reserved, manifestly fearful. That they served also as guards was obvious, though any attempt at escape would be foolish. Finding a way out from this wilderness would be as difficult as making a way in.

Shenandoah's assistants lost no time in setting about duties already assigned; to bathe her, coming the rich flame of her hair to added luster, providing choice foods. These things were external. Shenandoah sensed in the atmosphere a compelling, uncanny influence. She was a priestess, a superior being, accorded reverence as well as respect; glimpses of the acolytes, skulking at the fringes of the little meadow where her house was set — a lumbering bear, a fox-faced creature, the horns of a cow — fearsome and unreal, they were a horrible background of unvoiced menace.

On the second day she guessed that some sort of drugs, medicines compounded by the sorcerers from ancient lore and ritual, was being added to what she ate or drank. There was no taste, no

outward or immediate effect, but a sort of
lassitude, accompanied by strange dreams; illusory
fantasies troubled not only her sleep but her
waking hours.

On the third day she was taken before the
Bear — rickly clad in a beaded dress of soft white
buckskin, with matching moccasins on her feet,
an added flame of autumn flowers braided in her
hair. Mrs. Pedersen was left behind. She was
escorted by her maidens, almost as richly clad,
led by a secluded path to another sudden open
place, and there was the Long House, not to be
mistaken.

Nearly a hundred feet in length, the walls were
high and windowless, built of logs and bark. The
original long houses had served as communal
shelters in winter and inclement weather, warmed
by fires but almost insufferable from smoke and
the mingled fumes of close-packed humanity and
dogs, of drying skins and all that pertained to an
existence resembling hibernation but lacking the
boon of deep sleep. Neither the houses nor those
who inhabited them could endure the strain
more than a few years, after which new ones
would be built at a fresh location.

This house was hardly more than a symbol, in
token of the once undisputed power of the
Nations, now of this inheritor of an ancient
priesthood. White Bear, the Son of the Sun,
stood alone in front of the Long House to receive
her.

Shenandoah felt a sense of awe, accompanied

y disbelief. He was not at all as she had
pictured. Of medium height and figure, splendidly
but not heavily muscled, naked to the waist, a
white bear reared on his chest. He had the aspect
of a scholar, a dreamer, rather than a warrior, but
in the sharp probing gleam of his eyes she sensed
that he might be terrible.

And those eyes were blue, not black. And his
skin was as white as her own, scarcely tanned or
touched by sun!

He eyed her with a cold impassiveness which
seemed to strip the garments from her body, to
reveal her very soul. Even before he spoke, she
sensed something of the power, the magic which
he not only professed but exerted.

"The green-eyed prophetess of the scarlet
hair!" he observed. "Born to interpret, to
prophesy! And woe betide the tongue which
fails of clearness or speaks falsely!"

Shenandoah's head tilted proudly. She had
been stunned, almost frightened, but the threat
kindled a matching anger.

"I am neither priestess nor prophetess, and
how may I answer riddles which you may set
me? Or is it that, in your eagerness to provide a
show for others, for the ignorant and gullible,
you are interested only in that and not at all in
truth or its discovery?"

Since both spoke in English, it was doubtful if
any of the others, lurking close enough to hear,
could understand. But her mein, the contempt
and defiance in her tones, was not to be

mistaken. Her pride and arrogance matched th
Bear's.

White Bear stared, between anger and surprise
throwing back his head. Even as she spoke
Shenandoah sensed her mistake in judgement
Like most fanatics, this man deceived himsel
believing his own doctrines, and by that forc
impelling others to belief. The incredible, eve:
the impossible, was a necessary part.

As with Doorley, power was a heady potior
The Bear was not one to brook defiance, and h
would never recognize or admit his ow
shortcomings. She had made a bad beginning.

"A priestess of the royal clan sees visions, an
reveals what she beholds!" His voice wa
compelling, sharp not alone with anger bu
menace. "Listen well, Priestess, and heed! On
who fails — fails the Bear — dies!"

Swinging short around, he strode away.

Chapter Twenty-three

A mounting frenzy was taking possession of the group in the clearing below, a blood-lust such as drives coyotes or weasels to wild slaughter. Wild Horse's pronouncement had been translated, and it had shocked and dazed Doorley's captors. Enraged but hesitant, they had been temporarily checked.

McQuade's coming had removed the barrier. If there was to be a quarrel between the leaders, that was no concern of theirs, so long as they were free to run as a pack.

Montana watched, appalled but fascinated, fingering his bow and wishing that it was a six-gun, though the arrows had advantages in such a situation. A full quiver, like a belt fully studded with cartridges, would have altered the odds. Lacking both was invitation to disaster.

He was not surprised at McQuade's reaction. Jealous hatred had marked the relations between Doorley and McQuade from the outset. Not only was McQuade enraged that an Indian had responded to a plea which he had refused, but it pleased his vanity to assert a greater authority among the Indians than even so great a chief as Wild Horse.

With an eye to what was to come, the breakfast cook-fire had been kept alive. It smouldered at a safe distance from the stake and the wood piled around its base and the legs of Doorley.

Tied securely to it, the strain of the ordeal had etched furrows in his face, but Dorrley maintained a defiant spirit, upright on his feet rather than slumping in his bonds. The main difference was that hope, which for a few minutes had lightened his face, had faded. His eyes were dull, and he did not seem to hear the taunts and insults, or notice as painted figures capered and darted, striking with hands or switches. Blood stained his cheeks, a smear extending like a gash below one eye. But the other, blackened, swollen, remained defiant.

His refusal to cry out or grovel was having an effect. Gradually the frenzy quieted, the petty assaults slackening. They paid him the tribute of a brave man.

Bitterness rose like heartburn in Abbott's throat. For his own part, he would probably have a choice of dying speedily, after saving Doorley from the flames. A single well-placed arrow would be enough, and more than sufficient to renew and double their frenzy. He would be riddled by a return shower of arrows as soon as they sighted him and in any case the plunge of half a hundred feet would be fatal.

To alleviate Doorley's torture and die with him would be an honor if not a privilege. But the compensation for both of them would be scant; and worst of all, with his death would vanish any hope for aiding Shenandoah.

The dilemma was as sharp-pointed as the horns of a longhorn, made worse by sight and sound of the creek at the edge of the clearing, thirst adding to the cramping confines of his position. Excitement at the point of madness gripped everyone on the ground, all attention centered on Doorley. None thought to look for possible trouble in the branches above.

More men were arriving, five white renegades so well mounted that the earth-bound Indians scowled enviously.

Matching their compatriots, the newcomers were painted, half-naked, but Montana sensed a difference. Like himself, they had once been soldiers, and ingrained habits were not soon forgotten. Riding tiredly, their eyes quickened at the prospect of diversion. With no one to order otherwise, they decided to join the throng of

207

watchers.

All were hatless, heads shaven except for a braided scalp lock in emulation of the Indians; that would be as much for self-protection as arrogance; these playmates among whom they had cast their lot could turn from scratching to claw and rend.

Black stain, applied as a dye to what remained of one of the renegade's hair, had faded, leaving it a dirty yellow. He showed a good soldier's consideration for his horse, turning to loosen the girth and pull off the heavy saddle. The horse exhaled a gusty sigh of relief.

Before loosening the cinch, the yellow hair thoughtfully removed a couple of packets from behind the saddle — twins in size and shape, wrapped in stained canvas, and obviously heavy. He deposited them at the foot of another tree, opposite Doorley and the stake, a score of feet away.

From long habit, Montana classified them for what they must be. Powder and ammunition was usually brought up for a battle in additional quantities in horse-drawn carts. But under conditions such as these, with no carts available, supplies were often transported on the back of a horse. There would be powder in one packet, musket bullets in the other.

The care which was given them seemed pretty well to confirm the guess.

Half-consciously, Montana took note, most of his attention drawn as by a magnet to the stake.

The preliminaries had been dragged almost to the breaking point, beginning to exhaust even the patience of those in charge, while they relished each facial expression, outcry or plea for mercy which might be wrung from a victim. Anticipation was often a worse torment than the culmination.

But Doorley continued to prove a disappointment, as stoical as any Indian, his only pleas having been directed to a pair of leaders, one of whom had refused, while the other had promised help which was shown now as beyond his powers. Otherwise Doorley had hardly flinched. What he might do under the fire was to be discovered, but they had come to the conclusion that anything short of that was a waste of time.

Montana tensed, then shifted position for a better view through the intervening branches. A flat-nosed warrior, squat as a bullfrog, was assigned the honor of carrying flame from the freshened cook fire to ignite the other. A sudden hush had fallen.

The fire-maker was in no hurry, savoring his role, his moment of importance. Montana quickened to a sudden inspiration, a possible chance for counter-stroke. The odds were long but no more than any of the others which offered scantier return and with no greater a risk. Something which might work, if he could handle it right. And what he required was now at hand.

The necessary equipment was on his person or

in hand, or conveniently on a branch of the tree alongside his head. Working fast, schooling himself to steadiness, he pulled off strips of tinder-dry bark, wood which had received the full blast of summer sun, still retaining a degree of stickiness from formerly oozing pitch.

Enclosing the tip of an arrow with bark, tying it in place with a few inches of fish line, was comparatively easy. Over it he smeared fresh pitch from another point, higher up the tree. His attention was divided between the work and the flat-nosed warrior.

For both of them, this was their moment. The squat man stooped with unexpected grace, fingers gathering several flaming brands, a smoky collection as he came upright, face scowling in a dreadful intensity.

Montana fitted his arrow to the bowstring, drawing it back. The target below, almost straight downward, would not be difficult. He scratched a match, sucking a breath of relief as it flared. The pitch-smeared tip of arrow flamed, then was burning as it coursed, a winged torch, to thud into one of the pouches so carefully set apart by the yellow-hair.

Chapter Twenty-four

Montana's breath held tensely in his lungs as he awaited the outcome. At best it was no more than an even chance, since the flame might be snuffed out in flight, or even with a direct hit on the target, it could fail to penetrate the sacking or ignite the powder. But burning pitch was not easily quenched, and its hot breath could scorch.

Opposed to the favoring aspects were the odds, not quite even, that he might have picked the wrong target, so that the arrow would hit among leaden pellets instead of powder.

But that was not too high a hazard. He had handled enough similar packages to know the difference. Bullets, in such quantities, had a way of flattening from their own weight, spreading the container. Powder was lighter and fluffier, less likely to set solidly.

The squat warrior had reached the stake, his own brands in hand. Still pursuing the common policy of dragging out the suspense, he paused an instant, waving the torch mockingly before the dazed eyes of his victim.

A shattering roar sent both bags leaping, torn to instant fragments by their contents. A wild eruption of dirt and shrapnel musroomed across the clearing. Like the flaming tail of a comet, the bursting container of powder showered over the onlookers who had drawn back to escape the heat of the other fire.

A triumphant, gobbling shriek of triumph had trembled on a score of tongues, waiting only on the engulfing of the stake. It rose in an altered, frenzied tempo, consternation and terror in a reversed torment. As the rising fog of smoke started to dissipate, objects lay outstretched or writhing. Some were recovering, to crawl or run in a blind impulse to escape the unknown. Fully a half were unmoving.

Montana reached the ground, descending with a reckless speed, almost falling from cramped muscles. Such fear would not last long, and could not be wasted. Doorley, held in place by his bonds, stared dazedly, not yet understanding what had happened. But he had been at the far side from the powder, and what was better, the burning sticks dropped by the torch-bearer had scattered to the side, not among the brush around the stake.

A quick look around showed Montana what he needed, a tomahawk beside a limp brown hand. It needed only a few swift strokes of the blade to have Doorley loose.

Still bewildered, but accepting such reprieve instead of questioning, Doorley was able to manage a staggering run with Montana's assistance. Just beyond the larger clearing the horses pranced and snorted, tied to convenient trees. Their owners, who had arrived so usefully for Abbott's purpose, had been engulfed in the disaster or subsequent panic, blindly fleeing the carnage.

They helped themselves to the nearest animals, untying and scrambling into saddles. Luckily for Doorley, his cayuse quieted at the approach of a man. Montana's fought to break away, bucking before it would run, still frenzied with unseen terror, the sickly stench of blood and powdersmoke.

Montana scarcely noticed. By comparison, a seat in a saddle atop a bucking horse was luxury after the long strain of a tree crotch.

Men able to run were actuated by the single impulse, to get away. Even with wide-open eyes they ran unseeingly. Picking a course away from the increasingly used trail, Montana had no trouble in avoiding a few stragglers.

A mile beyond they reached what he judged to be the same creek, and halted to slake the thirst of men and horses. Montana's was less parching than on that occasion in the desert, but no less impelling. Doorley, who had endured even longer, thrust head and arms into the water, reveling in its wetness. He was gradually coming to understand what had happened.

"I don't know how you managed, Mr. Abbott," he admitted soberly. "Talk about a last-minute reprieve!" Not nearly so certain of himself as had once been the case, Doorley extended a hand. Montana gripped it hard, but silently. The gesture confirmed the need for going stealthily. As they remounted, there was a faint sound of voices, somewhere out of sight.

Panic would give way to a sullen anger, a desire for revenge. And others, making for the common destination, would be more than normally alert.

Philosophically, Montana accepted such luck as they were accorded. A reasonable freedom of movement, with horses under them, was a vast improvement over what they had experienced. Still, he'd hoped to find guns and other supplies on the saddles, a wish not fulfilled.

He still had his bow, which in that particular crisis had served better than a six-gun. Back at the clearing he's paused enough to snatch twice his former supply of arrows from the spilled fingers of a warrior whose need for them had passed and gone forever.

The trail gradually improved, careless signs of

passage easy to read, made by men no longer particularly concerned with hiding their presence. After all, what was there to apprehend, with the Long House almost within reach, where the Great Bear and his potent if fearsome powers must afford sure protection?

Since that logic did not apply where they were concerned, Montana turned the horses up another stream, following along its bed for half a mile, emerging when scant sign would be left. Some of the hurt would find themselves able to travel, felled more by fright than injury; noting the absence of their sacrificial captive, the slashed ropes, they would understand. Rather than an accident it had been a rescue. And now Doorley prowled these fastnesses, and there would be others with him.

The creek had angled away from the common trail. As the shadows lengthened and merged, hurried by the all but impenatrable wilderness, they came to a spot where he could detect no evidence that any man had been before. Both were drugged by exhaustion, but hunger was a continuing protest. For a man who enjoyed his meals regularly and often, Montana reflected, he seemed to miss far too many.

"We'll take turns sleeping, the other standing watch," he said. "I'll take the first." Doorley was heavily asleep almost before he could stretch on a deep carpet of leaves under the wide spread of evergreens.

Fishing served the double purpose of helping

keep awake and providing food. Abbott hadn't lost any of a small boy's pleasure in the eager strike of leaping trout. The closing dark put a stop to the sport, though by that time, with twice the usual number needed by a meal for twice as many men, he judged it sufficient. He used the last glimmers of light to gather dry wood, cleaning the fish mostly by feel and habit. The sheltered deep of a nook hid all firegleam even as the trees clothed the smoke.

The soft whispering of the stream matched the stealthy movement of four-footed creatures or the glide of owl or night bird. One single, tentative hoot he classified as belonging to the owl rather than a two-legged prowler. The aroma of roasting fish was a sharply pleasant pungency against the nostrils.

Abetted by hunger, it wakened Doorley, blinking with amazed incomprehension at this man with whom he companioned. Montana's estimate of provender proved accurate. There was enough, but with none left over.

Montana fished again in the dawn, the trout eager as before for any sort of offering. Hunger provided the savor lacked by salt.

"I take it that, like the rest of them, we're heading for the Long House?" Doorley asked.

"The Long House it is," Montana agreed. "Since we'll be traveling in the same direction, it will be at least as safe as any."

"We've both reason enough for wanting to reach it," Doorley conceded.

Prudence dictated that they wait out the day, before venturing to move again, but both were too restless. Increasing numbers would be already at the meeting-place, the Bear equally impelled to haste, the making of medicine, the final climax in which the prophetess would be called upon to interpret dreams, to read signs and omens.

Men of different tribes, most of them foes of long standing, would view each other mistrustfully, despite being on neutral ground rendered almost \holy by the presence of the Messiah for whom they had looked, who commanded peace among them. He would be urged not alone by his wish to launch an attack against all whites, but by the certainty that, unless engaged in such a common purpose, his troops would get out of hand. There was no time to waste.

They took time for one necessary rite, gathering berries, mud, the smear of certain pungent leaves, dancing and painting each others' faces and upper bodies, Montana making use of what Running Wolf had showed. With shirts stripped away, they would pass for renegades as easily as most.

The sun was crowding not alone the high peaks but its zenith when Montana stared in amazement at a distant mist which stained the sky to the south and east. Though dissolving as it ascended, that it came from more than one or even many small fires he had no doubt. Such action was a token of supreme confidence or carelessness. He found this disturbing.

Doorley had seen as well. His mouth twisted wryly.

"Now who would be that crazy? I'm not leading anyone — and almost any guide or scout should know better."

Montana liked that touch of wry deprecation. He was coming increasingly to like Captain Doorley. Some varieties of corn were slower than others in ripening, but almost always the quality was better.

With the smoke, there was a whisper, faint with distance, lost, pulsing again; a sound he'd heard too many times to mistake. Guns. But whose or what they might portend was anybody's guess.

Holding to a steady pace, he had an even surer sense that others were on the march, and quickening their own, in a contagion of expectancy which mounted toward excitement. Whether it was of expectancy or apprehension was another matter.

Thunder growled in the distance, as unusual as it was belated, but a gather of clouds above, dark as the wilderness below, confirmed it. Above them the sun rode undimmed, with no spatter of rain

The sun was still strong but westering when the forest thinned and they pulled up to stare in a matching excitement. Ahead were the fringes of a settlement. Cabins blended with their background, almost at one with pitched teepees, these at half a dozen locations.

Horses grazed, eager after the hunger of the long trail. Men moved, restless rather than resting, with efforts to do so hampered by fresh arrivals. Some scattered on clearly urgent errands. The distant beat of a drum would be a summons.

Montana's hunch had never been stronger. Already it was THE day. The coming night would be one of decision and destiny.

Chapter Twenty-five

What they could hope to do was being even more hindered by circumstance than Montana had counted on. He had been only too well aware of the difficulties of his mission, having undertaken it partly from friendship, but mostly because any sacrifice which might avert a wide-spread of slaughter would be worth the price. Once war erupted as the Bear intended, women and children as well as men must die; in the end, the color of their skin would offer no protection.

If they could get close to the center of festivities, the stroke of a bullet or arrow might throw matters into confusion, leave the movement leaderless. Even if he died moments later as a result, such an accomplishment would be worth the chance.

Not that it would necessarily have to work that way. Amid such confusion, almost anything could happen.

But the likely presence of Shenandoah complicated a matter already far from simple. To destroy the White Bear could spell her doom as well.

The swelling ranks of those who were gathering was an advantage. Few knew many of the others. So long as they made no serious mistake, he and Doorley could move virtually unnoticed, even with a certain boldness.

The original Long House, lost to flames and antiquity far to the east, had been in a hidden, all but unapproachable vale, and the Bear had emulated the former pattern as well as possible. They moved with the darkness, and the rising moon, seeming centered above the Long House, was a signal for night-long festivities to begin.

Concealed by a clump of brush, they took up a position where they could see and hear.

A pair of mounds, man-made, shoulder high, grassed over, fronted the Long House. A higher stone was set between, clearly the altar of the Bear, in his role as a high priest. Ancient symbols of a perverted religion.

Drums began a beat, their solemn echo breaking against the forest and more distant hills. Shadows emerged from among great trees, and

Montana saw that these were the drummers, painted, fiercely terrible in aspect. They marched twice around the circle beyond the altar, then squatted to its left, with no break in the tempo or hollow beat. They were followed by other proud figures, their crested war-locks painted white, bodies striped in black and white, loosely clad in white blankets crossed with a crimson band. Chanting solemnly, they took up places behind the altar.

The rites held a curious fascination, differing considerably from the sun dance of the Blackfeet or similar ceremonies of most western tribes; clearly they were patterned as closely as possible on the former rites of Senaca or Erie, a supposedly greater medicine or potent magic than was known to lesser peoples.

More painted warriors stalked into view, seating themselves in a watching semi-circle, facing the altar.

Acolytes appeared, skulking, sniffing, questing — night creatures increasingly bold. Far off, in the forest, as though awakened by the din, night owls shrieked. Squaws came, timidly, squatting at the rear of the circle.

Doorley crouched close, and Montana felt his start as a file of slender maids came dancing into view, moving toward the altar, naked except for a fawn-skin from waist to instep. They too, were painted garishly, and would in all likelihood have dreams which they would wish interpreted. Such matters, pertaining to ancient and once-innocent rites, were a necessary preliminary to the real business of the gathering. Everything was designed to impress and over-awe, to weld warriors of differing tribes to a common purpose, affording the White Bear a total dominance.

More maidens came, some clothed in a feathered dress of white, others still more strangely; then a pair, wearing crimson masks, struggling for all their litheness to drag the carcasses of two great hounds. These they deposited in front of an increasingly hot fire, as its flames drove back the shadows.

There was increased singing and chanting, words cried loudly which clearly held great meaning. A heavy-set warrior, scowling and intent, long knife in hand, followed behind the dogs. Clearly an acolyte, he disdained the animal likenesses of his companions, bending to slash and disembowel the dogs, shouting, casting their entrails into the fire.

It was grimly impressive, a token of what was to come. The effect, upon minds conditioned to savagery and the words of a prophet, could not but be profound.

Hands dripping blood, the warrior raised to more than his full height, balancing on tip-toe, his high shriek dreadful as a panther's. In response, the acolytes quested in ever wilder frenzy. Montana's nerves were taut. If they should come prowling among the bushes –

Another girl danced into sight, beating a small drum. She was clad in blue feathers beneath a scarlet head-dress, and she led a howling procession of warriors, who moved to stations to the right and left of the mounds.

Sudden silence fell as another figure appeared, moving slowly, shrouded almost head to foot in a white dress, above which her hair reflected the crimson cast of the flames. Montana heard Doorley's sharp intake of breath. Like a sleep-walker, Shenandoah reached the altar, stood a moment in silence, then mounted the left-hand mound and seated herself, bowed head shrouded by a black hood.

Whether she had been drugged or otherwise conditioned, or was acting a part demanded of her and on which her life depended, she played the role with consummate skill.

A final figure came into view, well apart from others — The White Bear. There was no mistaking who or what he was, though he was clothed and painted in scarlet, all save his face. That was untouched, pale and aroogant. Clearly a throw-back to some white ancestry, he made that an advantage rather than a handicap, playing upon it.

The acolytes came capering, fawning about his feet. He ignored them. Others watched, silent and fearful. Disregarding everyone, he reached the altar, placing upon it a scarlet bow and red arrows. He was at once the White Bear and the Scarlet Priest.

His attention held as were the others, Montana discovered that another man had somehow materialized, unnoticed until he loomed threateningly impressive in his own right. Wearing black feathered plumes, his body painted an equal jet, he mounted the opposite pile from Shenandoah. His bow and arrows were black as the surrounding night.

Deliberately he strung the bow, setting a dark arrow to the string. Still facing the Witch Woman, the prophetess, he seated himself.

"Good God." The whisper was torn from Doorley. "He's there to watch her!"

Much of this might be play-acting, to impress the spectators. Most was grimly real. Other tribes of the original Six Nations had turned away in loathing and disgust from the perverted rites of the Cat People. Now the White Bear boasted of descent from them, that he was the last priest of an ancient line. Zealous in his dream of uniting all red men, of sweeping whites from the land, he was not hesitating at reviving forbidden customs. Montana suspected that he might add a few refinements of his own.

The arrival of the executioner was a signal. The acolytes flanked the Bear on either side. Shenandoah lifted her head, as if rousing from meditation. She shook her head, and her long hair fell, clouding her to below the waist in a flame-filled shadow. The Bear swung to face her.

"Prophetess!" He spoke in English, but his voice rang. She, of course, would understand no other tongue. For the throng, it would be even more impressive, and in any case he was contemptuous of them; they were mere instruments to his purpose.

"I have dreamed that the Moon Witch must be clothed, she and her daughter, against the coming chill of the winter. But with what shall they be clothed? I have dreamed. Interpret this to my people."

Shenandoah responded slowly, her voice without a quiver, head still bowed. Only one white arm lifted, pointing.

"Two dogs lie there, their fur soft and deep. Paint them with the sun and the moon. So shall the Moon Witch be clothed, the dream of the Bear come true!"

This, apparently, was the approved answer, from ancient, more innocent times. Just as clearly, it was not the one which the White Bear desired.

"Shall I not instead offer the Moon Witch and her daughter the soft skins of young maidens — such as these?" He gestured where the girl with the drum, alongside a scarlet-clad maid, stared and suddenly shrank back in terror.

A sigh which was more a groan rippled through the onlookers. This was what they had hoped for, a sacrifice to the sun and the moon, to assure victory in the coming struggle. Their mood would not be content with symbolism.

Shenandoah did not look up. Her voice was unruffled but certain.

"The great dogs wait. Their fur is soft and warm for the Moon Witch. It is the custom."

Whether or not the White Bear had dreamed or merely day-dreamed, his plans were fixed, and this captive woman was defying him. His tones were cold with meance.

"Customs change. I have dreamed that the soft skins of maidens shall provide the clothing! Look closely, Witch! Do you not behold them, strangled upon this stone?"

The girls cowered away, but there was nowhere to flee. Even their companions, light-hearted in pretense once moments before, would not dare lift a finger in their behalf. Shenandoah's voice was still unmoved.

"You have dreamed, O Sachem. I have interpreted according to the signs. Would you have me lie?" Glaring angrily, the White Bear looked significantly at the executioner.

"Perhaps we both have read the sign wrongly. Would another soft maiden's skin – a white skin – be more fitting?"

The drums had fallen silent, silence taut as a bow string. Shenandoah's head lifted proudly, returning glance for glance, but she disdained to answer. Controlling himself with a visible effort, the Bear swung to the waiting maidens.

"Speak," he commanded.

Almost frantically, the dancers raised bare arms, crying out on cue. "We have dreamed also, O Bear of the White North! Let the sorceress explain our dreams!"

One sprang to the front, terribly in earnest.

"O prophetess, last night I dreamed! In the

228

hills was the sound of thunder, then the roar of falling water, and at sunset a red cloud!"

The answer startled even Montana.

"As water falls, so do men. Out from a leaden hail is death. It's thunder was in your ears, and in the cloud was reflected the red of blood!"

However ambiguous, her interpretation was convincing, more terrible in its implications than in what was stated. The red priest swung furiously.

"Executioner! Set arrow to bow!"

Chapter Twenty-six

Doorley gave a strangled cry, the sound covered by the half moan of anticipation which swept the circle. He seemed on the point of hurling himself blindly at the Bear when Montana grabbed his arm.

"Hold on to yourself," he warned. "A wrong move would insure her death."

Doorley seemed to awake, as though he too had dreamed, but nightmarishly. He nodded comprehension.

The executioner brought his bow level with his eyes, fitting an arrow, drawing the string to the tip. But Shenandah was faster. Drawn to her full height, flinging back her hair, she gave the Bear glance for glance.

With hand half-lifted for the signal, he returned her look, while silence reclaimed the meadow. The fire had died to a bed of smouldering embers, but the moon cast a white brightness. Even the drummers had come under the spell.

Whether Shenandoah was responding to the power of suggestion and the influence of drugs or potions, or if she was imbued as the signs and portents had indicated, entering into the wild spirit of the occasion, she played her part with a matching abandon. It was the White Bear's eyes which fell, not her's — a bare flicker, but enough.

"Have a care, Witch," he warned thickly. "A false prophetess shall die! Make sure that you interpret truly what my people dream."

"Why should I lie?" Shenandoah asked. "The dreams are not mine. Should truth be set aside, the interpretation would indeed be a mockery."

Her voice was strong, with no quiver, her green eyes flashing in challenge. An ember flared, reflecting the flame in her hair, the cat-sheen eyes.

Montana's own bow was drawn, the arrow aimed for the unwitting executioner. He had been sweating, but he was suddenly as cold and deadly as the warrior. The chief difference between them lay in the distance which the arrows must travel, for the space between the mounds was less than half what Abbott would have to shoot.

But if the Bear signalled, he intended to beat the black killer to the shot. This was vastly different from confrontation with a sixgun, but the same principles of reflex coupled with sureness applied, and Montana had no doubt that he could outmatch the other.

What would follow then would be the bad, unpredictable part. Momentarily it would save Shenandoah, but even if he managed to fit and loose a second arrow, even to bury it in the throat of the Bear, the crowd would spring to madness

By slaying the Bear he might accomplish the purpose on which he had set out. No one else would be able to seize leadership over so motley and restless a throng. A dozen chiefs would vie for power, and almost certainly end by warring among themselves. The Bear's dreams and purpose would die with him.

Shenandoah understood her peril, the risk in defying and thwarting the man who considered himself not along prophet but messiah. But she was undaunted.

"O Bear," she said. "Let your executioner send his shaft winging — if you dare! Well do I know that it is poisoned, though such a thing is alien and forbidden in all the traditions of the Long House! Never has a priest of the Long House dared doubt the prophetess who reads the dreams! Doubt — and die!"

The red priest stood bewildered, appalled in turn. Clearly he had not expected any opposition from this captive woman whose life as well as her welfare depended on serving him in this role to

233

the best of her wit and ability. That she had been uncooperative at the outset had been understandable, but under the influence of carefully chosen attendants, along with potions, and most of all with increasing understanding of her helplessness, he had had no qualms.

She might stumble or bungle her role, but he had not expected defiance. All at once his own belief was on trial. He had elevated her to an ancient but powerful role, and if she was indeed a prophetess, a sorceress according to the signs and portents by which she had been chosen.

If she was speaking truth, out of conviction as well as certainty —

His own certainty was shaken, but he was saved the need for a choice. Shenandoah seized the initiative. Turning, she swung to face the shadowy throng, and her voice carried like a bell.

"Listen, O Warriors of the West, gathering to your own destruction at the call of a false prophet!"

Montana started, between admiration and understanding. He was beginning to sense the depth and courage of this woman. Given a power rooted in tradition and superstition, she was making full use of it. She could not know, or hardly suspect, that he or Doorley or the Sachem might be near, but she was staking as much on a single throw as he had been prepared to do, hoping to disrupt the impending attack, to set tribe against tribe, at least to a smouldering hostility.

How much she was influenced by potions and the power of suggestion, how clearly she was able to see and interpret the dreams, she was as daring as anyone.

"This Bear who is white, O Warriors, calls for the interpretation of what has been dreamed! And shall he or you be denied the vision? Not far to the east are dead men, their faces buried in the rotting leaves of the forest or the dust of the open plain! Many lie dead, some in coats of blue, others in paint or feathers. There is thunder among the hills, flame in the forest!

"I see streams running red, even at midday. There is battle and death, the trampling of feet in wild flight, the sound of guns, the rattle of swords! Men stumble and fall, and do not rise, and their blood reddens the thirsty soil. As your Sorceress I am compelled to speak what is there to read, to warn you. Men, many men, wearing blue, march ever to the west!"

Terrible in his rage, the White Bear had tried to interrupt, and failed. He started to signal, and Doorley cried out.

"Kill that man!"

For once, Montana was beaten to the draw. Then, as others were doing, he started, startled, appalled, then began to understand.

There had been no sound, or at least it had gone unheard above the whispering murmur running through the uneasy spectators, but the black hand of the executioner had been pierced by an arrow, which pinned it to his own bow.

That unseen arrow had sped so swiftly that no one understood, nor for an instant moved. Then the stricken warrior screamed, a high frenzy between pain and terror, clawing and wrenching at the arrow which nailed the bow to his palm, dripping with blood.

The Bear stood frozen, eyes shifting from the screaming executioner to the immobile prophetess. The warrior, normally disdaining to show any trace of fear or pain, had been terrified beyond all control.

"Is this your power, Witch, your accursed magic?" The Bear screamed. "Dare you pit your witchcraft in opposition to mine? To strike thus when threatened! You shall burn! Take her — "

His voice broke on a croaking, strangling note, sheer amazement on his face. A second arrow quivered in his throat. With it rose the triumphant war cry of a voice which Abbott could not mistake. The Running Wolf, Sagamore and priest in his own right, had avenged the desecration of the ancient religion, visiting his anger upon an infidel upstart.

Chapter Twenty-seven

Amid the wild blare of excitement the Running Wolf's shout was virtually unnoticed. Then there was a conflicting noise, an insistent murmur, distant sounds which had been covered, unheard while the immediate drama was being enacted. Hard on the heels of its warning running men broke from the shroud of trees, stumbling, staggering with weariness — men in panic flight, who had come close to the limit of endurance. Warriors, smeared and faded paint and tribal insignia denoting several nations, but no longer proud. They were the remnants of a defeated army. Clearly, on their way to the rendezvous, intent only on what lay ahead, some had forgotten to guard their rear. The surprise which they had intended to inflict had fallen upon them.

That accounted, at least in some measure, for the distant smokes, the whisper of guns. Whether Shenandoah had glimpsed and interpreted, or dreamed indeed, her prophesy was in process of fulfillment.

Soldiers had come out of the east or north — contingents despatched much as he had been, hopefully to arrive in time. Well led, probably with more than a bit of luck, they had disrupted the remnant of those who came, impelling those able to escape to greater speed, to tidings of disaster.

In the annals of war that would probably go down as a minor engagement, but beyond question it was proving decisive. The White Bear was dead, not by the hand of a white man, but by the avenging stroke of one of his own people.

His dream had come within a fraction of at least initial success, inspiring diverse tribes to gather and join in some sort of federation. That in the end it would probably have split apart over native hostilities scarcely detracted from the initial triumphs of the Bear.

Failure heightened the peril of Montana and Doorley, Shenandoah Mrs. Pedersen and Running Wolf. Expectancy was succeeded by panic. Here was the proof of disaster, as the prophetess had foretold, but such grim sorcery of one termed Witch and accursed rendered the sullen warriors doubly savage. The ruin of so bright a dream was not easy to accept.

Montana fought his way toward Shenandoah, standing beside the altar. Alongside the fallen Bear, she was still surrounded by a huddle of her maidens. Instead of guards as well as attendants, they now beheld in her the incarnation of the priestess, prophetess and witch, who had dared defy even the White Bear.

Doorley was ahead of Abbott. Shouting wildly, he wrestled a war-axe from a dazed warrior, then, striking right and left, cleared a way. He reached the altar as others shrank away, and Shenandoah was in the shelter of an arm, looking up at him between amazement, relief and other emotions too overwhelming to understand.

Again there was interruption, a roaring laugh, brittle and harsh as a rattlesnake's warning, overriding the confusion. McQuade had remained as silent as others while the ceremonies mounted to climax, but was moving now to reach Shenandoah, undoubtedly to provide such protection as he might in the seething madness.

Reaching her in time to see her sheltered by Doorley's arm; one more jolting surprise in a night of disaster.

Nothing quelled McQuade for long. Like others gathered for this night, he had dreamed dreams, to watch them shatter, and the final hope, compounded of a greater madness, gone even more devastatingly. In the face of that he laughed, but it grated, holding threat beyond mirth.

"You again, Doorley," he bellowed. "And in my way, as usual — and just in time to die!"

His six-gun was lifting as he spoke. The whisper of an arrow might have gone unheard at any time, certainly in that moment when the night rang with pandemonium. Even McQuade's gasping cry, as the revolver slipped from nerveless fingers was all but unnoticed. Blood reddened his shirt front. With the fingers of his other hand he plucked clumsily at the arrow quivering in his chest.

Wild Horse, bow in one hand, wrenched McQuade around with the other. Despite the collapse of his hopes, the chief was grim-smiling.

"We've an account to settle between us," he reminded. "A mounting one, and it comes first." Wasting no second glance on Shenandoah or the sprawled figure at her feet, he marched his prisoner away.

Looking after Wild Horse, the shadow of a smile eased the grimness of Montana's mouth. His bow was suddenly useless, his last arrow used, still quivering in the back of the acolyte whose legs threshed in final gesture, his wolf's-head mouthing the earth. His hurled tomahawk had missed Wild Horse, diverted, falling short, unnoticed by the chief. The arrow's speed had saved not only Wild Horse but Doorley, even if neither would ever know.

Montana scooped up the dropped revolver. It had a comfortable feel to the hand.

Nearly everyone was running, succumbing to blind panic. No one paid attention as Doorley and Montana formed an escort for Shenandoah, but for once she was unsure of herself or of direction in the darkening night.

"We must find Jememiah," she insisted. "She was left at the cabin. I can't go without her."

"This way." Running Wolf spoke from beside them. He was the Sachem, smug, as purringly triumphant as the cats his people despised. Long as the trail had been, for him its end left nothing to be desired. "It will be better to wait there, with her," he added, "while these dark places are emptied of frightened but dangerous fugitives. Presently the soldiers will arrive."

A great dark shadow still loomed. "One thing remains," Running Wolf added. "Do you still have a match, my friend? It will be quicker, and easier."

Montana supplied it, then helped gather grass and brush to pile at a corner. They stood back to watch the mounting flames of the Long House, scarlet against the night sky.

Gun Law In Toledo
Wes Harding

Spawned by the Spanish conquistadors, the town of Toledo had become nothing more than a small, sleepy little cow town (or so it seemed on the surface). Sheriff Tom Howard found plenty of time to look after his own TH Ranch as well as administer what passed for justice. But when the saloon keeper, the lawyer and the slim, cold-eyed man with a gun came to town, the lazy pattern of Tom's life was blown right into a rain of lead.

12516—$1.25